The Branches of Time

First volume

by Luca Rossi

GW00776715

Contents

Contents 3

1 5

2 7

3 9

4 13

5 16

6 19

7 20

8 22

9 26

10 28

11 30

12 33

13 34

14 39

15 44

16 48

17 51

18 54

19 56

20 59

21 62

22 66

23 69

24 74

25 77

26 79

27 83

28 87

29 92

30 96

31 100

32 103

33 105

34 108

35 111

36 119

37 123

38 127

39 131

40 133

41 134

42 138

43 141

44 143

45 146

46 149

Galactic Energies 153

The Branches of Time – Volume II 155

The Author... 157

1

Why does she keep flirting with that moron? wondered Bashinoir, the best man.

Ignoring her husband's disapproving looks, Lil continued trading coy smiles with Anodil, a man ten years younger, standing tall in his handsome green suit.

"...to be your lawfully wedded husband?" asked the priest.

The pure white snow fell softly over the guests and the trees of the forest. Several women shivered from the cold. The freezing temperature didn't seem to bother Lil.

All of a sudden a mass of dark shapes darted through the snowflakes. The priest stopped in mid-sentence. Bashinoir watched him waver and then fall backwards, his forehead split open by a sharp shard of stone. A shower of razor-sharp pieces of rock hammered down over the guests. Covering his head with his cape, Bashinoir ran towards his wife.

Men, women and children fell to the ground. The blood seeped through the snow, forming red haloes around the cadavers. Bashinoir grabbed his wife's hand and continued running, pulling her behind him. She tripped and fell. Bashinoir picked her up, lifted her over his shoulder, covered her with his cape and dashed towards a gully in the rock. It was just big enough for Lil to take shelter, as her husband protected her by stretching his own body over the opening. A vortex of screams, wails and sobs whirled behind them. A shard lodged itself into Bashinoir's calf. The blood began gushing out of the wound.

The voices grew quiet. The shower of rock shards had stopped. Bashinoir lifted his head and studied the area around him. "No, don't look up," he ordered his trembling wife. Bodies were stretched out all over the ground, torn to shreds and floating in a lake of blood.

Bashinoir helped Lil to her feet. She pressed her head against his shoulder, covering her eyes with her hands. Husband and wife headed towards the Temple. He was limping. They passed by a shapeless hunk of flesh, wrapped in a green garment soaked in blood. Bashinoir held his lady even closer. They reached the sacred building. Standing in the doorway, the priestess Miril observed the massacre.

"Black magic has fallen upon our island," she said. "Come in."

"Did any others survive?" Bashinoir asked in a weak voice.

"No. Just you."

The three huddled around the sacred fire. They were the last inhabitants of the frigid island of Turios.

2

None of the three wanted to break the silence. Despite the sacred fire, they didn't feel the tiniest bit of warmth.

Bashinoir stared at the flame. He observed Lil's face out of the corner of his eye. She was staring at the ground, still trembling slightly. Tears streamed down her face. Bashinoir thought about young Anodil. A surge of jealousy shot through his body, yet he immediately repressed it. He wanted her to explain why.

No, it's not the right time, he reasoned. He couldn't let jealousy get the better of him right now. In his mind's eye, he watched the shards of rock fall from the clouds yet again. The priestess had said something about black magic. *But why? What did we do to deserve so much cruelty?*

Lil couldn't hold back her tears, though she wanted to put up a brave front. *I have nothing left. Everything's gone. They're all dead. My island no longer has a future*, she agonized.

Friends, relatives, parents. The blood of everyone she loved had poured into that red lake staining the snow outside of the Temple. When they walked to the Temple through the expanse of cadavers, not a single moan had come from that pile of bodies without souls.

Alone!

There were just three of them left now, on an island forgotten by both humans and gods. "Maybe...maybe we should go back and see if anyone survived," she suggested through her sobs.

The priestess and Bashinoir looked at her. Neither said a word. Bashinoir thought about what he had seen in the snow as he and Lil headed to the Temple. The cadavers on the frozen blanket of snow were nothing more than shapeless heaps. The pointed shards had lacerated their limbs and torn strips of their flesh away. They no longer looked like human beings. No, none of them had made it out. Bashinoir didn't want Lil to go back and see those bodies again. He would rather wait for the following day to go out and burn them himself, alone. He silently hoped it wouldn't snow much over night: then it would be easier to bring the bodies to a woodpile and burn what remained of the people he had shared his life with.

Absorbed in his own thoughts, he absentmindedly sighed, sadly: "Ah..."

The priestess noticed Bashinoir was still losing blood from the wound on his calf.

"Bashinoir, come with me. We have to dress your wound. We need to find a warmer place. After we take care of your leg, we'll try to eat something." She knew none of them would be able to swallow anything down.

Bashinoir, supported by his wife, followed the priestess. He had never before been granted entry into the Temple quarters.

"Wait. Just a minute. I need to see something. Don't move. I'll be right back," the man said.

Lil and the priestess watched him limp away.

Outside, the snowfall had grown into a blizzard that blocked the weak light of dusk from shining through. Bashinoir could barely see his hands in front of his face. The blood stains had already been covered by a new layer of snow. He noticed the depressions created where the bodies had fallen to the ground. *But where are the bodies now? Where could they have gone?* He groped his way through the storm and reached the nearest depression.

He knelt down, feeling around the snow with his bare hands. No, it wasn't an illusion. The body had disappeared.

Could it have been blown away by the wind? Impossible!

He searched around the stain, looking for marks or signs that it had been dragged away. But he didn't find a thing.

How much time had they spent in the Temple, standing around the sacred fire? If anyone had survived, there's no way they would have had time to drag away all of the cadavers. There weren't any footsteps, either.

He stood up, looking for another depression. Nothing, no bodies. Exhausted and in pain, he continued searching. He fell down to the ground, then pulled himself back up. He knew he was still losing blood. He stumbled towards the trees. He peered into the forest but couldn't make out a thing.

I need to go back to the Temple. Now.

He turned around and headed back. A few yards away from the entrance, he fell to his knees. He tried to get back up, but his legs no longer obeyed him.

"Come, Bashinoir," the priestess whispered. Her silhouette blurred into the flurries swirling around in front of him. Then everything went black.

3

"Close the door and come help me," the priestess Miril ordered Lil. Struggling with the man's weight, they carried him to a room adjacent to the entrance and stretched him out on his stomach over a skin that covered the floor. The priestess removed his boots and pants. Lil tried to hide how awkward she felt.

The wound was very deep. Miril left the room and came back with a small box. Once the wound was cleaned, she took out a needle and thread and started to stitch the skin back together. Then she covered her handiwork with a bandage.

"Listen, Lil. We won't be able to carry him to another room." She told Lil where to find wood and the other skins. Lil left, coming back with what they needed a few moments later. They lit a fire in the hearth and created a bed with the remaining skins. Bashinoir's forehead was burning. "I'll go make him an infusion. Wait for me here."

On her way back, as she passed by the entryway, a strong gust of wind slammed against the heavy wooden door, blowing it open. The storm invaded the foyer. The priestess stopped, stunned.

"What happened?" Lil asked, rushing over. She followed the direction of the priestess' gaze. Lil turned towards the open door. The two women stood as if they were waiting for someone or something to come in. "Help me close it," Miril urged her.

Staring at the door panel opened to the right, the priestess moved forward. Lil paused for a few seconds, then, her eyes locked on the opening, imitated Miril with nervous, cautious steps, heading instead towards the left panel. As she pushed, she felt as if invisible hands on the other side of the panel were exerting a pressure against her. *That's impossible. I'm just tired.* And yet it seemed as if Miril was struggling as well. *We're women, this is the kind of thing you need a man's muscles for.* The focused, tenacious eyes of the priestess gave her the energy she needed to dig her heels in and push. Her body shook, her muscles screamed, but finally the panel yielded shut, just as Miril also succeeded in overpowering the other panel.

Could that wooden barrier keep them safe? Could it really protect them from the evil that had devastated their home on that ill-omened day?

Lil tried hard to convince herself that they were safe now.

Miril and Lil looked after Bashinoir until, exhausted, they collapsed onto the cushions arranged in front of the fire. His fever was under control. The wound had stopped bleeding. He was breathing normally.

"Priestess, can I ask you something?"

"Miril. Call me Miril. There are so few of us left. Perhaps formalities are no longer necessary."

Lil couldn't hide her astonishment. A distant and inaccessible figure, the priestess had always embodied mystery. Lil had only come close to her during the most important rituals. They said she spent most her life shut up in the Temple. Whenever she left, searching for some plant or mineral, Lil would watch the priestess walk along the paths of the island, alone. Nobody dared say anything to her. The Elders called upon her from time to time to settle disputes they were unable to resolve themselves. The priestess' judgment was always accepted with absolute obedience.

Rather abashed, Lil continued: "M-Miril, I wanted to ask you, if you could tell me, what do you think...what happened?"

Miril studied the girl's black eyes. Lil felt her gaze penetrate deep into her soul. It seemed as if the priestess had only then noticed her presence.

She really is gorgeous, Miril mused. It was hardly surprising that most of the island had admired this maiden's attributes. Her limbs were perfectly proportioned. Her complexion was dark, her frame petite. The contours of her face were flawless, and her dark hair spilled down over her shoulders in graceful curls.

"I'm sorry, Lil. I don't have an answer yet. I sensed a very strong black magic. I doubt the wizards of Isk are able to manipulate that kind of energy or command the elements so effectively. Yet...I still don't have an explanation."

Miril felt slightly guilty. There was so much more she could have told Lil, but only she and the priest could know those secrets. Since their people had come to the island two thousand years ago, the priests were responsible for handing down the truth of their past. The Elders, however, told the people only part of what had happened through a few different legends. The truth was too dangerous. They were convinced that ignorance of their own past would protect them, allow them to build their new homes and continue on with their new lives.

But now something had gone terribly wrong.

Did our protections fail? What can I tell her? Miril wondered, as the girl's questioning eyes peered at her.

"Lil, do you know why our people live on this island?"

"I know that our forefathers came here from far, far away, because the land where they lived before was freezing," Lil rattled off unceremoniously.

"That part is true. The Northern lands were no longer habitable, so our ancestors traveled over the seas to find a new place to live. When they found this island, they decided to settle down and prosper. What else do you know?"

"Not much. The Elders don't like it when people talk too much about the past. They say it's better to focus on our work."

"Lil, what you know is the truth. But it's only a part of the truth. The rest is not so easy to explain."

Behind them, Bashinoir stirred. Miril and Lil went to his side. His forehead was burning. His fever had returned.

The priestess quickly left the room to prepare another infusion. Lil wiped the sweat from her husband's forehead. Upon Miril's return, they woke him up so he could drink. Bashinoir moaned. He tried to speak but was only able to grunt. Miril and Lil continued tending to him until the fever came down once again.

Finally, in the darkest hours of the night, the two women barely had enough strength left to drag the cushions in front of the fire. The priestess didn't want to return to her own quarters and leave the man and woman alone.

"Lil, take these cushions and put them a few feet away from the fire. We can sleep here tonight. Tomorrow we'll try to carry Bashinoir to a more comfortable place."

Lil did as she was told. Miril headed towards the cushions, carrying a skin. It was the only one left in that room. She gestured for Lil to lie down next to her. Somewhat reluctant, Lil stretched out along the priestess' side. Again, she felt embarrassed, but soon the fatigue accumulated during that long day came over her and she fell asleep.

Miril admired the perfect lines of Lil's face.

How could something like this have happened? She had never

felt an energy as strong as the one she had felt that day. There was no question in her mind that the dark influence had come from the Northern lands. So they hadn't stopped looking for them after all. After so many years, the lords of those lands still nourished an insatiable thirst for revenge.

I need to get some sleep. The next few days are going to be very long indeed. She glanced over at Lil's face once again. *She really is beautiful,* she thought.

4

"We can escape from this island," Anodil said.

"Are you crazy? What's come over you? You know full well that we shouldn't talk about those sorts of things," Lil retorted.

"Even if we shouldn't talk about them, we still can. Who said we have to stay here forever? We can keep it a secret. I could build a boat for us to sail away. If our people managed to come to this island, then it must be possible to leave it!"

Lil's hand caressed the bark of a tree trunk. Her gaze was lost in the leaves.

"Anodil, I...I wouldn't go with you. This is my home. This is where my parents are, where my brothers, my sisters, my friends live. And...my husband!"

"But you don't love him. Don't lie. You love me!"

"That's not true. I don't love you. I am and I always will be faithful to my husband."

"Lil, your parents forced that marriage on you. You can't bear to be around him. It's written clearly all over your face, every time I see you two together."

"I told you that's not true!" Lil interjected, immediately wishing she hadn't raised her voice so much. She looked around, afraid that someone had been listening to their conversation. "Stop it, just stop. I'm leaving!"

She started off but Anodil grabbed her arm, stopping her in her tracks. Lil shook him off violently, losing her own balance and falling against a tree, scraping her elbow.

Anodil came closer to help her but Lil brusquely stepped back, then continued on her away.

"Lil, don't leave. Please!" Anodil implored her. Lil turned around to look at him. Wounds oozing out streams of blood appeared across the boy's face. Lil flinched, horrified. Anodil held a hand out towards her, as if asking for help. A shard of rock pierced through the flesh of his arm.

"We can escape. We can go together. We can get out of here. We can love each other. We can escape..." Anodil repeated, in a macabre singsong, falling to his knees. His skin was already almost entirely covered with blood. A dark stain spread out across his shirt.

Lil wanted to escape, but she couldn't get away from him. As she backed away, she tripped over a root, falling to the ground. Anodil, moving forward on his knees, came towards her.

"We can be together forever, in a marvelous place..."

Lil wanted to scream. She opened her mouth but no sound came from her lips. Anodil's body was almost next to her own. She couldn't move. The arm he held towards her suddenly broke off. His hand and forearm fell at Lil's feet. A heart-wrenching scream exploded inside of her.

"Lil, wake up. It's just a nightmare."

The girl's eyes flew open, meeting the concerned gaze of the priestess, just a few inches away from her face. She felt her body and face drenched in sweat.

"Lil, it was just a dream. It's alright. We're in the Temple. You're safe."

Lil looked around her. The flames crackled cheerfully in the hearth. She turned towards her husband and couldn't hold it in any longer: she burst out sobbing. In that moment, the tears she had been trying to hold back all day long, as she strived to match the strength of the priestess and her husband, exploded in a delirium.

"Go ahead and cry, Lil. It'll do you good."

The young woman couldn't rid her mind of the horrible images from her dream, all muddled up with scenes from the wedding that had been transformed into a bloodbath. Once again she saw the thousands of piercing shards fall from the sky as human beings were transformed into deformed, bloody heaps of flesh.

Miril softly hugged her and Lil started to calm down, now somewhat stunned and ashamed.

"Everything's going to be alright. Don't worry," Miril whispered softly. "Let's try to get some sleep. The sun will rise in just a few hours, and we have lots of work to do tomorrow."

Lil laid back down, as did Miril, who pulled her close in a gentle embrace. Lil laid her head on the priestess' chest, who caressed the young woman's hair.

"Things will work out. We'll be just fine. You'll see."

Lil's eyes were still open. Feeling the priestess' hands upon her made her tense up. After a few minutes, however, fatigue once again got the better of her and she let herself surrender to the embrace, the caresses, and sleep.

5

The morning light came bursting through the Temple windows. When Lil awoke, the first thing she noticed was the fire crackling in the fireplace. She looked around for the other two. Her husband was still asleep. The priestess was gone.

She rose to her feet and headed towards Bashinoir. His bandage had recently been changed; Miril must have already taken care of him. She left the room and headed towards the sacred fire. The heady fragrance of incense hung in the air. The priestess was sitting in front of the flames, meditating.

"Come here, Lil."

"Pardon me, priestess. I didn't mean to disturb you."

"I asked you to call me Miril yesterday. Don't you remember?"

"Yes, I'm sorry...Miril."

"No apologies are necessary," the priestess replied, smiling.

Yet again, the memories from the previous day washed over her. Lil burst out crying. Miril walked towards her.

"Lil, don't worry. We'll find a solution."

Miril had been saying the same thing to herself since she had awoken at the first crack of dawn.

Everything will be alright. We're within the Temple walls, after all. Nothing can happen to us here. Whoever did all of this probably can't even sense us. They won't care about a measly three survivors. If they've spent all these years looking for a way to take revenge, then they're probably satisfied now. But what if I'm wrong?

"Miril, I have to worry. They're all dead. All of my family. There are just three of us left on an island that has no contact with the external world. What are we going to do? How are we going to stay alive?"

"I know, Lil. It's not easy. It seems as if the gods have forsaken us. But if this is the destiny they chose for us, we must accept it. This is our trial. Now calm down. Try to relax."

"My husband still hasn't...woken up!"

"No. I'm afraid he's lost a lot of blood, he's quite weak. Unfortunately, you and I are the only ones who can bury the bodies now."

"But -"

Lil wasn't at all sure she would be able to handle that. Yet again, yesterday's horror flashed through her mind. How could she bring herself to touch those bloody hunks of flesh, which the nighttime frost had probably already frozen into stiff, ghastly postures?

"I'm frightened, too. But there's nothing else we can do. Those people deserve their funeral rites, and we can't leave their mangled bodies lying outside the Temple, at the mercy of the winds and the wild beasts."

Help her burn the body of every person she had ever loved in her life. That was what the priestess was now asking her to do. The young woman would never have dared to question the priestess' orders. And now, reluctantly, she acquiesced, muttering in a faint voice: "As you wish."

Miril smiled at her sweetly. "We'll get to that soon enough. Come with me. I've prepared a lovely infusion for you."

Somewhat hesitant, the two women moved towards the main door of the Temple. The priestess had changed into work clothes, something Lil had never seen her dressed in before. She offered Lil a change as well. They both moved clumsily, hampered by the weight of the heavy leather garments.

"It is time. May the gods be with us," Miril said before flinging the heavy wooden doors open.

Awestruck, the two women stared at the scene in front of their eyes. Neither was able to speak. The space in front of the Temple was immaculate, a pure white blanket marred only slightly by the tracks of a few small animals here and there.

"How could..." Lil managed to squeak out.

The priestess didn't reply. She walked down the Temple stairs straight into the snow. The sun shone in the sky and the chilly wind nipped at her skin. Lil stood standing in the doorway, watching Miril.

Moving very carefully, the priestess dug through the snow in several places before finding what she was looking for: a stain of blood in the lower layers. Yes, a body had fallen there, in that spot.

But where is it now?

She looked around, suspicious, as if someone or something was going to jump out from the trees. The forest appeared to be calm. The snowfall had wiped away every trace of horror from the

17

previous day.

"Miril, where are all of the bodies?" Lil whimpered. The surreal stretch of pure white snow was even more ghastly than what she had prepared herself to see.

"I don't know," Miril answered, coming back towards her. "Let's go back into the Temple."

The two women immediately felt safer after closing the door behind them.

But it's not the wood that's protecting us, Miril thought. After she woke up that morning, she had renewed the protection spells. No, the dark forces couldn't reach them here, in this place.

"Miril. Those sharp pieces of stone that fell from the sky - what were they?"

"I can't really say. I'm sorry. I haven't had a chance to start looking into it."

"And the bodies? Where did the bodies of all our people go?"

Miril shook her head. "Lil, I don't know."

She's the priestess! How could she not know?

Miril felt the tension in the girl's eyes. She looked at her gently, moving closer and taking her hands in hers. Lil stiffened.

"We will find out the truth. We will find out what happened. Don't lose faith. If the gods wanted us to be saved, there is surely a reason why. So please, keep calm. Nothing bad can happen to us here, in the Temple."

Lil wasn't convinced.

We'll have to leave here sooner or later. We'll have to find food, go hunting, go collect our things. And whatever killed the others will be able to do the same thing to us.

Miril studied Lil's worried face. She trailed her fingers along the sides of the girl's body, then behind her back. Lil's body grew even more rigid. Miril embraced her. Lil wanted to melt into that embrace, but something wouldn't let her. The woman standing in front of her was the priestess. Before now, she had never so much as spoken a word to Lil.

Miril broke away. "Go see how your husband is faring. He may very well regain consciousness soon."

6

"Are they all dead?"

"Yes, my Lord. The rite has been performed and your orders were carried out exactly as instructed."

Beanor felt a deep sense of satisfaction. He rose from his throne and moved towards the window. He looked out over the sea, as if he could see the island in the distance.

"And you are, of course, aware of the fact that absolutely none of them must survive under any circumstances whatsoever?"

"Of course, my Lord. Your orders were very clear. What we unleashed upon them did not spare a single soul."

"And you are aware, wizard, that if this proves to not be the case, you'll pay for it with your own life?"

Aldin swallowed. Anyone who failed to make the king happy usually paid the highest price.

Beanor continued looking out over the sea. A grin slowly spread across his lips. *All dead.* It was over. The force that had constrained them to these lands had finally been broken. Now they could board their ships, take to the seas and explore new lands. After two millennia of immobility, they could finally set out upon the routes traced across the ancient maps.

His shoulders were covered with a fur wrap. His nude torso was unaffected by the freezing air. The crown of his head was bald, the long hairs of his neck and sides swept back into a ponytail. Beanor's hand moved towards his hilt. If that wizard had messed up again, if he had to lose more ships while trying to get over the barrier, he wouldn't kill him. Oh no. He would torture him for years, then let him heal, then torture him some more. He would reduce him to human larva and make him rot in prison, just like those who had failed before him.

"Very well, wizard. Now that the curse and the barriers are broken, call the generals together to prepare the warships. We have no way of knowing who we'll run into on these new lands."

I, too, will be on one of those ships. And, if the gods will it to be so, I'll never come back here, the wizard Aldin thought to himself.

7

Heady aromas wafted through the air around the sacred fire. The priestess Miril was sitting on a cushion, staring at the fire. Lil, exhausted, slept in the room near the entrance. Bashinoir still hadn't stirred. After resting and being tended to all day, his health seemed to have stabilized. His vital energies were growing stronger.

Miril closed her eyes. Images of the fire continued to burn through her mind. She slowly separated from her own physical body. The fire shrouded her entire being. The priestess was now nothing but flames. She started to feel herself rise, higher and higher, until she saw her own body sitting, meditating, back down on the floor. Then she looked up. She rose even higher, moving beyond the Temple's archway, until she floated freely in the air. The freezing gusts had no effect on her spirit. She looked up and the starlight made her feel even closer to the gods.

She continued to ascend, until the island was but a speck beneath her. She imagined she was a falcon and dove towards the forest. Before reaching the crowns of the trees, she turned back up. She flew over the woods and mountains. She circled around and studied every angle with her bird's eye. Nothing. She didn't see a single soul on the island. She moved beyond her sense of sight and tuned in to her other faculties of perception. Those souls, just a day after their death, should still be connected to their physical bodies. She tried to detect their presence, yet didn't feel a thing.

Then she plunged into the depths of the water surrounding the islands. If they weren't on land, for whatever reason she would eventually discover, then they must be in the sea. She moved along the ocean floor, exploring the underwater caverns. There was no trace of the physical remains nor the souls.

A tear fell down her cheek. Her body quickly called her spirit back to it. She regained control of her limbs, allowing the heat of the flames to console her, caress her face, and thanked the gods for the powers they had granted her.

It was her duty to protect them. She was the one who had to take care of those people and their children. That was what she had been born for, what she had been prepared to do. Years of suffering, studying, and rituals. She felt like she had never really lived. She had dedicated every second of her life to studying and practicing magic. And for what? Her spells should have kept the island hidden from the eyes of the dark forces.

And yet they had been found. She had felt the magical forces coming from the North just a few moments before the violent storm of stone shards had burst out over the island. She had run out to warn them, to call them into the Temple, since, at least between those walls, they could have been protected.

But she hadn't gotten there in time. Her words had died in her throat. She had seen them fall like leaves. Some had been ripped to shreds as they ran to seek refuge in the Temple, falling as their eyes, begging for salvation, stared at her.

Only Bashinoir and Lil had made it. As they ran, it had seemed as if they were dancing under that hellish rain, as if every shard had casually landed just a little bit ahead or behind them. As the two walked into the Temple, a stretch of lifeless bodies stretched out behind them outside the Temple. She had heightened her senses to seek any vital signs in that multitude of cadavers, but found nothing. Locking eyes with Bashinoir, she understood that the man had also realized the truth: none had been saved. If they had survived, they would have to fend for themselves.

Miril rose to her feet. She wanted to go back to her quarters, but decided instead to look for Lil and Bashinoir.

They were both sound asleep. Lil's breath was as light as a little girl's. The woman was no longer quaking from her nightmares. The priestess moved closer and gently caressed her. She lifted the skin covering her and laid down next to her. Her energy drained from performing the rituals, she embraced the girl and let the sweet sensation lull her.

Sleeping next to another human body. She had never done such a thing before the last two nights.

8

The wizard Aldin waited for the boy, who had just left the hotel, to turn the corner. He carefully listened for the sound of his stumbling footsteps. The young man entered the alley without noticing the shadow crouching in the darkness. Aldin let him pass by and then jumped to his feet. He grabbed him from behind and, with a dry movement, twisted his head to the right. The boy crumpled and slid down, but Aldi hurried to keep the body from falling to the ground.

"No, come on. You can't get your spiffy soldier uniform all dirty." Grabbing the body by the shoulders, Aldin dragged it a few feet and propped it up against the wall. He checked to see if anyone else was coming down the alley, then took a key out from his pocket and, opening a small wooden door, slipped inside, dragging the cadaver along.

Stooping over the body, he tore out a lock of the boy's hair and placed it in a luminescent purple vial placed on top of the table. He pronounced the words of the spell and waited. A few minutes passed silently as Aldin watched the fluid in the vial whirl and gurgle, soon emitting a faint wisp of smoke which grew to the size of a man as it spilled out onto the ground. The smoke coiled around in the air, becoming thicker and thicker, developing a texture and changing color, from gray to light pink. Feet, ankles, legs, pelvis, chest, arms, backside and finally a human head gradually formed. The lines became more distinct as skin and hair also formed.

Aldin glanced over at the dead soldier. The fluctuating simulacrum in front of him had the exact same appearance. *But it still needs a soul.*

The wizard jumped forward, as if diving into a pool of thermal water.

He immediately noticed the powerful strength of the musculature, the young and strong arms, the firm legs, the clear vision and acute sense of hearing.

He ran to the mirror and rejoiced in the image it reflected. *Excellent, Aldin. You make quite the handsome little soldier...*

He knelt over the cadaver. After undressing it, he dragged it to the furnace in the adjoining room. He hoisted it up to the hatch and pushed it inside. The flames devoured it. *Very well.* He got undressed and threw his own clothes into the fire. Returning to the other room, he put on the uniform. He wrinkled his nose at the odor. *It wouldn't kill these soldiers to use a little soap every once in a while. Well, now's not the time to be too picky.*

As dawn broke, Aldin and the other soldiers filed onto the ancient warship. Lying on his cot, he rubbed his hands. He couldn't wait to be one of the first to leave this land.

Freedom!

He was finally a free wizard who could roam the lands of this world, no longer yoked to serve that homicidal maniac of a king. *Just a few days' journey and then...*

The ship left the dock. Soldiers and sailors hollered at their loved ones standing on the pier. They were to be the first men to leave this land in ages. The freezing wind failed to impede the women's determination; they waved at their men crowding the side of the ship, intent upon seeing them off until they were far in the distance.

Aldin noticed one girl in particular staring right at him. He looked around, but the soldiers next to him were all looking somewhere else. He looked at her, somewhat uncertain, and she seemed to get angry. Then the commotion came over him: "I'll wait for you!" she yelled, trying to overpower the rest of the voices and conversations. "Come back soon! And bring me something from the Southern lands!"

Repressing a sneer, Aldin lifted his hand to wave at her as he forced his lips into a smile.

After two hours of sailing with the wind at the stern, the sailors bustled about as the soldiers chatted and drank.

"We're there!" the look-out cried. Tridis was just a mile away. It was little more than an exposed reef but, for over two thousand years, no ship had ever been able to cross this impassible limit.

The captain paced up and down the deck with his hands folded behind his back.

"We're there!" he repeated to himself. All of the sailors and soldiers were now on deck, their eyes trained on the reef as it grew closer and closer.

"What if that royal wizard was wrong? What if the barrier hasn't really been broken?" a sailor asked softly.

"What are you saying, asshole? There's no way he could have made that kind of mistake," another replied.

"Yes, but...the other wizard, the one before, he said he had succeeded in doing the same thing. And nothing but a few pieces of wood ever came back from those other two ships," the first continued.

"You son of a bitch, are you trying to curse us?" the other accused him, coming forward with his fists raised.

Aldin jumped in between the two men. "Relax. Don't worry. The first wizard was just an old drunk, and the king made sure to punish him good."

The two soldiers stared at him, suspicious, but Aldin had diffused the tension and they all went back to join the other men watching the reef as it grew closer.

Now close to Tridis, the captain ordered them to haul in the sails and throw down the anchor. Three rowboats with six sailors and a helmsman each descended. The boats headed south over the choppy sea, effortlessly managing the waves.

The only sound heard on the ship was the lapping of the tide against the reef and the seagulls flying above, occasionally diving into the water in search of food.

The rowboats grew smaller as they moved further away. *One mile*, Aldin counted. *Two miles!* he counted later. An irrepressible wave of exultation chased away every dark doubt in his mind. *The barrier's gone. I put an end to two thousand years of isolation. And soon, I'll be free!* He wanted to jump gleefully and embrace the other sailors, who were still waiting, holding their breath.

When the rowboats were over three miles away from the ship, the captain gave a signal to the look-out, who blew his horn. The entire crew was swept away in an explosion of joy. For a few fleeting moments, the hierarchy was broken, rivalries disappeared, and divisions between men faded. Officers, sailors and soldiers hugged one another and celebrated as a single man, whooping and shouting into the sky. Even the cries of the birds flying above them seemed to be in the same spirit. Reckless in their revelry, three men fell overboard, soon helped back up by their mates. Even a timid choir sang the praises of King Beanor, whose people had now reconquered the freedom to plow through the seas.

Finally, the ranks were reformed and the captain gave the order to lift the sails. The ship seemed to fly across the waves. Three miles along, the men and rowboats sent as scouts were collected and the race with full sails resumed towards the South.

After a few hours of light-hearted navigation, the bowsprit, the wooden beam upon the prow, came crashing down. Then the figurehead was crushed by an invisible force.

The sound of the broken wood echoed in the hearts of the men. The prow started dissolving into smithereens. The ship, pushed along by the impetuous wind, smashed against the invisible barrier. Soldiers and sailors crowded the deck. Some jumped into the water. The back of the ship, still afloat, quickly started to sink, dragging down the men who held on tightly to the balustrade.

Aldin was in the water. He tried to cast spells that would keep him alive and give him warmth. But no words came out from his frozen lips. He grabbed on to a piece of wood. He looked around: the screams and pleas for help were no longer echoing out into the sky. The water was full of inanimate bobbing objects, which were human beings just moments earlier.

Did I fail? Is it my fault they're dead? he asked a few seconds before his own heart stopped beating.

9

King Beanor poured wine down the cleavage of the girl lying at his side in the gigantic bed. The liquid traveled towards her navel and Beanor leapt up to lick it. *Soon wine will no longer be a luxury for just a select few. We'll grow vines in warmer lands. We'll fill swimming pools full of it.*

His tongue traveled up to her breasts. He closed his lips on a nipple and savored its taste, as if it were the sweetest of fruit. The kind that barely grew on this cursed land. He pounced upon her lips and bit them until she struggled to free herself.

"Your Majesty!" the young woman protested.

"Did I hurt you? Little whore!" he insulted her in reply.

"No, not at all, your Majesty. Please, I beg you, continue," the frightened girl pleaded, offering him her bloody lips.

Beanor hastened to suck up the drops of blood. He closed his eyes, inebriated with the flavor.

Someone knocked on the door.

"Who is it? Don't you know that I'm busy?" he yelled hoarsely.

"Your Majesty, I have an urgent message."

None other than Tuirl, my incompetent advisor.

Beanor got out of bed and pulled on a pair of pants.

"Come in!"

The prostitute covered herself with a sheet and moved to slip away through a service door.

"Where do you think you're going? I haven't finished with you yet. Get under the covers and try to stay warm, you slut."

She obeyed without uttering a word.

Tuirl looked down, visibly embarrassed.

"So? Speak! Or are you waiting for my cock to grow completely soft?"

"Your Majesty, a few pieces of the ship that set sail three days ago have washed up on shore," Tuirl exhaled all at once.

Immediately livid, Beanor let out a disconcerting scream that shook the walls of the palace.

The eyes of Tuirl and the girl darted about, panicked. Beanor flung the candlesticks to the ground, then grabbed a sword and swung it at everything around him. Tapestries, curtains, furnishings, nothing escaped the wrath of his fury. He stopped for a second, exhausted.

With blood-shot eyes full of hatred, he stared at Tuirl. He took a step towards him as Tuirl retreated.

No, I need that imbecile.

He turned around and strode towards the bed. He lifted the sword over his head and slammed it down with all of his strength, cutting several inches into the wood underneath the mattress. A clean, precise slash. The girl's head rolled across the floor.

10

Beanor sat on his throne, nervously drumming his fingers against his arm.

Tuirl stood facing him. Old, almost bald save for a few short, white hairs, he was weathering yet another of the monarch's rages.

"So, advisor. Tell me again what you're insinuating – and this time be clear about it, unless you want me to throw you down into the castle dungeon."

"Your Majesty, the court wizard, Aldin, has disappeared. The only possible reason we've found to explain his absence is that he decided to join the crew on the ship."

"That bastard!" Beanor exploded, his face purple. "How dare he board that ship without my permission?"

"Your Majesty, if something did go wrong, what prospect awaited him here? He knew what would have happened. As he was reasonably sure of the efficacy of his magic powers, he probably thought the best choice was to leave."

"That dog! What a useless piece of shit, a joke of a wizard! How could he even think to defy my will?"

Tuirl patiently waited for the king's fit of anger to blow over.

"Speak, by the gods above! Must we stay confined to these frozen lands for the rest of eternity?"

"Unfortunately, with the departure of Aldin, the only wizard left in our court is young Ilis, the apprentice, who hasn't had enough time to complete his training. But..." Tuirl paused for a moment, afraid what he was going to say would incite the rage of the monarch once again. "But, Ilis could mature under the guidance of the former court wizard."

Beanor let out another roar. The veins on his neck seemed ready to pop: "Advisor! Have you lost your mind? I locked that man up twenty years ago after his failure cost me three good ships. The only reason I still keep him alive is so I can continue to torture him. What use could he possibly be to us?"

"Your Majesty, I'm afraid that it's him or nothing! He did indeed make an awful mistake, but he's the last chance we have!" Tuirl explained, the words coming out all in one breath.

Beanor leapt forward to attack the advisor, who stooped down, trying to shield himself from the king's hot-headed reactions. Rather than beat him, the king calmed down at the last minute and whispered in his ear: "The only reason I continue to spare you is the promise I made to my father. Go get that filthy piece of shit. But if your little idea doesn't work, not even father's spirit will be able to save your life."

"As you wish, your Majesty," Tuirl concluded, turning swiftly to leave the throne room.

11

As Tuirl entered the dark cell, his eyes failed to detect any trace of a human being inside of it. Overwhelmed by an unbearable stench, he couldn't help but take a few steps back. A moan from the corner caught his attention. "Obolil, is that you?" Tuirl asked.

Instead of a voice, a barely audible, broken whisper answered him, sounding as if it belonged to a spirit: "The d...door. Cl...close it. The...light...blinds...me."

"Oh, sorry."

Tuirl's eyes adjusted to the darkness. The floor was covered with excrement and moldy food. *I can't stand it in here.* He felt faint. Tuirl immediately turned around and left. Once out of the cell, he ordered the guards to go and bring him the old wizard Obolil.

Supported by two soldiers, what appeared in the doorway was but the semblance of a man: all skin and bones, his mouth devoid of teeth, lips eaten away, filthy hair down to his knees, completely naked.

"You...you were my friend," the wizard mumbled. "And you let them do...all this...to me..."

Back in his office, Tuirl sat facing Obolil. He had ordered them to cut his hair and beard, to wash him and give him a warm meal. But the man in front of him was still a far cry from the wizard the king had locked away twenty years ago. Obolil struggled to hold on to the right arm of the chair.

But it was the old wizard himself who broke the embarrassing silence: "I assume the latest expedition didn't go too well."

"What do you know about that?" the advisor answered coldly.

"You don't need magic powers to listen. The guards are always chatting. And lately, that's all they've been talking about." He grew quiet, then resumed speaking: "So what, did you think that incompetent Aldin would manage to do what I was unable to?" It seemed as if Obolil's face were trying to smile, but all he could manage was a grimace of pain, which sent chills down Tuirl's spine.

"Aldin was sure he had found the right spells to break the barrier. He convinced the king to invest an awful lot in the search for minerals that are nearly impossible to find in these lands. For years,

30

men dug through the snow and the ice. Finally, when it was all ready, the rites were performed. And immediately afterwards, Aldin swore that he had incontestable proof that the barrier had been broken: that he had taken an astral voyage all the way down to the Southern lands. So the king sent out a reconnaissance ship.

"And then, my good advisor, all you got in return was a few sticks of wood floating in with the tide. That's what happened, right?"

Tuirl shivered, thinking of how the King had exploded when he had gone to tell him the bad news.

"The king loves to listen to those who tell him what he wants to hear," the old wizard continued, staring at Tuirl. "So, advisor," he continued, "what brought you to visit my cell, after twenty long years of silence?"

He'll never go for it, Tuirl doubted. *But he's the last card we have to play.*

"The king orders you to resume your duties at court."

Obolil's reply was a series of convulsive tremors. The advisor couldn't tell if this was a physical problem or if Obolil was trying somehow to laugh.

"Me, at court, taking orders from that creature? Tuirl, I think these past few decades have made you more demented than I."

"Obolil, I think it's in your best interest to accept. It's an order, after all. And if you don't agree, the king will order that the torture you were first subjected to be resumed yet again."

More tremors and starts. "Do you think that sort of thing was ever stopped?"

He has nothing left to lose and doesn't want to live anymore. I'm not going to get anything out of him.

"You'll get your laboratory back. Your library. Every object, magical or not, that was taken away from you."

For the first time, Obolil lifted his head, opened his eyelids and stared at Tuirl's face with both eyes.

"Everything?" he asked.

"Every single thing."

"And in return?"

"You'll have to teach the apprentice, Ilis, and make sure that the magical wisdom of our people is not lost. You need to help him gain the powers needed to try, in his turn, to open the barrier. He needs to succeed where you failed."

31

Obolil's head dangled from his neck as he shook it slightly, a stream of drool trailing down towards the floor. Grinning, he announced: "I accept!"

12

"That's not fair!" Ili protests, clenching his fists, his face red. He storms away, barefoot, across the manicured lawn.

Nal's smiling face suddenly transforms into a worried expression.

"Come on, Ili, don't quit. It's not unfair, it was just a good move!"

Ili turns around; his blond curls shade his face. "No! You said you wouldn't do that! Now I'm going to tell father."

Nal rises to her feet. The universal window the two children had been playing with, just a few feet high, now gracefully rolls up by itself and returns to the girl's ring as she catches up with her brother. He looks at her, sullen.

"Ili, you're distracted. You were caught up in their feelings and you lost track of the protections. But it's not over."

"You know how much I cared about that marriage!" Ili exclaims. A tear streams down his face.

"I know, but you need to learn that, even when we're excited, we can't lose track of everything else." The girl holds her hand out to her little brother.

"Sometimes I'd like to give them a world like this one; beautiful land, trees, birds that sing," he says, looking around him.

"Me too, you know. But the game has its rules. Want to play some more?"

"Okay," the boy responds, sitting down with his legs crossed on the grass.

His sister imitates him.

The universal window unrolls between them. In the center, the light reflected by an azure planet shines stronger than all of the other stars. Nal touches it gently with her thoughts.

13

The fire had gone out. A thin trickle of smoke rose from the embers. The room was flooded with light. Lil opened her eyes and realized that the priestess' arm was resting on her chest. Miril was still deep asleep. Lil had to go to the bathroom, so she tried to gently move Miril's arm. The priestess snorted and opened her eyes. Suddenly a giant smile spread across her face.

Why is she so happy? Lil wondered, perplexed.

"Good morning, Lil," she began, without lifting her arm.

"Good morning, Miril." That excessive closeness made Lil slightly anxious. *Where was she last night?* Lil had woken up several times during the night and hadn't seen the priestess. "I thought you had gone to sleep in your quarters last night," she commented, immediately regretting her insolence. She still felt rather uncomfortable talking to the priestess.

"No. I was just up late, working on a few things," Miril explained in a serious tone of voice, seemingly distracted. She suddenly seemed to be lost deep in her thoughts.

Miril must have slept only a few hours, but she didn't seem at all tired. Even her hair was neatly done. She was as beautiful as ever, with the intense gaze of her green eyes and the long, light chestnut mane that unfurled down her back.

Life had always been hard for everyone on that island. Lil wondered what it must be like for a woman who had never experienced the intimate companionship of a man.

A moan from Bashinoir distracted her from her own musings.

"Let's go see how he is," Miril gently urged.

He was still sleeping, apparently peacefully.

The two women checked his calf. Lil could barely believe her eyes: the wound, although very deep, looked much better.

Miril smiled: "Just a question of using the right ointments."

Lil anxiously waited for her husband to wake up. She wanted to embrace him, for him to take her in his arms, to sleep with him. Thinking about how, even so recently, she used to enjoy teasing him and making him jealous now made her feel terribly guilty. *But now I'm all his and only his, body and soul*, she though, bitterly.

"I think Bashinoir should wake up sometime very soon," Miril

34

announced.

"Miril, did you find anything out, while you were working last night?" Lil asked, astonished by her own boldness.

The priestess shook her head. "I'm sorry, Lil." She didn't think the girl would understand what an astral voyage was, but she still tried to explain it: "I went through the astral planes of the entire island looking for the bodies and their souls, but I didn't find a single trace. I even searched the bottom of the ocean, and even there, no luck."

Planes of the entire island? At the bottom of the ocean? What is she talking about?

The young woman wanted to know more, but she found it incredibly difficult to ask Miril more questions.

Luckily Miril met her halfway: "Don't worry if you don't fully understand what my words mean. I'll help you as much as I can. There are many things you'll be able to learn. Now come with me, let's go make breakfast. There's something very important I need to talk to you about and it's better that we don't waste any time."

And most importantly, Miril thought, *with Bashinoir asleep, Lil can make her choices more freely.*

Miril and Lil sat at the table in the dining hall of the Temple. For the first time, after the tragic events of the last two days, they had finally prepared a real breakfast with the best of what the island had to offer. However, they ate as little as possible: who knew when Bashinoir would be awake and able to hunt. Over the next few days, they were bound to see their food supplies dwindle.

As she ate, Lil's cheeks finally began to regain their color. Her black eyes moved from one dish to the next: she had never sat at a table laden with so many wonderful things to eat. The culinary customs of the people of the island were not even remotely similar to those of the priest class, which received the best of every kind of food, in quantities much larger than necessary for their needs.

Miril let Lil eat peacefully, without disturbing her. When it seemed like she was full, she decided to bring up the subject that was weighing upon her: "Lil, my dear. There are just three of us left on this island. We have no idea what set off the inauspicious events of the day before yesterday, but we are alive and we have to make sure we do all we can to continue this existence in the best way possible."

Lil was surprised by how serious the priestess sounded, and she listened carefully to every word. The priestess' expression still seemed gentle. She felt like the priestess was finally going to disclose something important.

"As you know," Miril continued, "the priest has left us, unfortunately. If I had been the one officiating the wedding, he would have been spared. But that's not the way things went." Miril seemed to be sincerely saddened by the death of the priest, although this meant she herself had been saved.

"You may have noticed that the priest and I never left this Temple together. Energy balances are very important. Since our people first stepped foot on this island, the priestly class has always had the duty to protect all of its inhabitants. In order for that to work, there always need to be at least two priests. Both receive the same teachings, so that they can work in unison and in symbiosis in order to perform the necessary rituals. Most importantly, so they can perform the protection spells."

Lil had actually never thought about why there were two priests.

"Do you know how a new priest is chosen?"

Sure, of course. It was the highest honor for a family to have a child chosen for the priestly life. Not only would the infant's destiny be changed forever, but the position of the entire family would rise to the highest level of the island's hierarchy, and the head of the family would be admitted as a member of the council of Elders.

"Of course. When a baby is born, the priests go to see it during the first few hours of its life and decide if it's going to become one of you."

Miril thought of how to make her explanations more accessible to the young woman. "You see, Lil, every child has their own energy current, an inherited trait and a predisposition that may be perfectly suited for the major powers and responsibilities that come along with the priestly life. Becoming a priest is not just a high honor, but first and foremost a heavy burden. The life of all of the inhabitants of this island depends on the protection provided by magic. If the priests fail, if they don't fulfill their duties, the consequences may be very harsh indeed."

So then it's their fault if... Lil started to wonder.

Once again, it seemed as if Miril could read her thoughts: "Lil, I can assure you that neither I nor the priest were ever distracted from our duties. What happened can't in any way be connected to a failure on our part. There must be another cause and, one way or another, I'll figure it out."

Is that a desire for revenge in Miril's eyes? Lil wondered.

"In any case, Lil, we will need to attend to many things over the next few days, including finding food, taking care of the animals and the fields, and checking the houses of all those who have left us. But the most important thing is that we need to be sure that the magical protections of the island are not interrupted, ever, for any reason whatsoever. In order for this to happen, there need to be two priests once again!"

Bashinoir! So that's why they were sitting in the kitchen, near the warmth of the hearth, the table laden down with all those delicacies. The priestess was trying to tell her that her husband would become a priest. *But priests...don't have wives! They don't sleep in the same bed as women. They dedicate themselves to the Temple, to the rites, to magic. They have practically no ties to their family of origin.* So the priestess was trying to tell her that her husband would no longer be her husband.

Her mouth hanging open, Lil observed the woman sitting in front of her holding a mug of milk in her hands. She couldn't help but feel a surge of jealousy. *Miril is so gorgeous!*

Tall and regal, Miril had a timeless beauty to her. She had always seemed so natural while performing the rites, her movements graceful, as if she were a creature of pure spirit. Even during those sacred events, Lil hadn't been able to take her eyes off the elegance of her gestures, made even more fascinating by the white veils of her tunic.

No, that can't be it. My husband is a clumsy lumberjack. Bashinoir could never take on such a role! But then, why was Miril talking to her about it? It wasn't at all necessary to ask for her permission: on that island, the law was written by the word and wishes of the priest, nothing more and nothing less. That was not about to change, even if there were only three of them left now. *Or maybe Miril is only trying to be nice to me, asking me kindly to step aside?*

The two women sat in silence for a few moments. Lil was caught up in her thousand and one thoughts. Her fingers lingered near her mouth as she nervously bit her nails. The priestess, from time to time, glanced over at her, smiling, a knowing look in her eyes.

"What do you think?" Miril asked her.

"Priestess...I mean, Miril, I...I really don't know what to say. Of course, your will shall be done, I mean...what you say goes. If you think Bashinoir should become a priest, I will accept that and I won't get in the way." A tear made its way down Lil's young face. "Yes, I'll accept it. As you wish, priestess – I mean, Miril." Now it all made sense for Miril to be telling her all of this: she wanted Bashinoir to be free from distractions, and that she, as his ex-wife, would prepare him in the best way possible to start down that spiritual path.

Miril smiled yet again. "Lil, Bashinoir will not be the new priest. You will."

14

The wizard Obolil staggered through the magic laboratory, leaning on a walking stick. His face wore a grim expression as his eyes darted quickly from one point to another. "Ah, Aldin, that fool! Look what he's done to this place. I wonder how anyone could get anything done with all this junk everywhere," he wheezed.

The apprentice Ilis stood in the center of the room, embarrassed, unsure of what to say, where to move, if he should sit or start cleaning.

"Absolutely nothing. He understood absolutely nothing, from everything that I taught him. Look at what he surrounded himself with. And he thought he could break the barrier with this?" he said, sweeping his arm along the table and knocking off a bunch of precious objects. "Throw it all out in the garbage! I don't want to see any of this crap any more!"

"But master..."

Obolil turned around to look at the boy, his angry eyes framed by dark circles.

"You'll speak when you're spoken to, boy. Do you understand me?"

"Of course, master," Ilis responded. He went to get a broom and dustpan in order to sweep away all of that *crap*.

Watching the boy leave the room, Obolil gave him another order: "Then come right back here."

Reluctantly, Ilis threw out everything that had been so carefully collected over decades of research and returned to his new master, moving towards the table Obolil had, in the meantime, taken a seat at.

"Sit down!"

Ilis obeyed.

"Give me your hands."

Obolil took Ilis' hands. The boy had to stifle a wave of disgust. The old wizard's body, despite having had a few days to refresh and reenergize, was still frightening,

His eyes were sunken in their dark sockets. His face, hands, wrists and every visible patch of skin was covered with scars. Only half of his right eyebrow remained. His fingernails were broken, split or completely missing. A segment of the pinky finger on his left hand was missing, just like his right earlobe. The wizard could not hold his body up straight. Even while seated, he slouched so badly that the top half of his chest was nearly parallel to the top of the table.

"Ah, I disgust you, don't I? Look at what our dear king has done to me! And that's the man I now have to serve. The man who rules over both of us, and he won't think twice about doing the very same thing to you if you don't give him what he wants." Obolil spoke in a very low and hoarse voice, interrupted frequently by short coughing fits.

"As for me, boy, I may not be here for very long. So if you want a different fate, you better be able to learn quickly."

Obolil closed his eyes, although his left eyelid remained open. He breathed in heavily: the air seemed to hesitate before entering his lungs.

"Do what I do. And stop staring at me with those frightened eyes."

"Yes, master."

Ilis bent his head down.

A few seconds later, a powerful energy began to flow from his right to his left hand. The sensation caught the apprentice unprepared, and he moved as if to withdraw his hands.

"You didn't even get to this level? Poor Aldin. He'd have been the last child in the world I would have ever chosen for an apprentice, if I hadn't screwed his mother!"

The energy flowed with an even greater intensity. Ilis felt himself catapulted into a vortex of emotions which inspired, alternately, happiness, fear, pure terror and joy.

"Surrender, boy. Don't try to resist."

Ilis tried to do as he was told but his body only stiffened further.

"I told you to surrender!" Obolil yelled at him, panting. Ilis thought the wizard was almost about to faint, so he tried to put into practice everything he had learned over those years. He relaxed his muscles and mentally recited a few formulas, releasing as much resistance as he could. The vortex of energy reached an unparalleled intensity. Suddenly Ilis found himself watching himself from above.

What in the...?

You've never done this before? Obolil asked him.

You can...

Read your thoughts? Of course! But only when we're out of our bodies.

Ilis felt himself getting sucked back down.

No, don't be afraid. Fear prevents you from advancing.

Master I...I don't feel ready.

Nonsense! I'm the one who decides if you're ready or not.

What do you want to do?

Obolil's voice came through clear and strong, his words articulate. Ilis realized that he respected that voice.

They tortured my body, but they could never touch my spirit.

Ilis felt slightly ashamed.

We need to try and work together so we can find more information. The island is the problem. Aldin could have spent the next few centuries digging around for precious minerals and still never have gotten anywhere. The barrier is fed by the rituals on the island.

But master, we used all the energy we had to create a cataclysm that would exterminate all of the inhabitants of the island. The master...I mean, Aldin personally went there to make sure his operation was a success.

Oh really? Let's have a look. Visualize yourself near the Tridis reef, on this side of the barrier.

Ilis tried, though he had never seen that place.

Concentrate. You don't need to focus on the place. Simply think that you are there.

Suddenly Ilis found himself above the sea. Hundreds of feet below, a reef was bathed in the foam of the waves. Obolil was at his side, incredulous and smiling.

Aldin, that poor idiot! Can you feel the barrier?

Ilis had no idea what to do.

Don't look so sad. You don't feel it because it's not here anymore. But if you concentrate, you can feel the weak force left. Follow me.

The wizard flew ahead, over the waves, followed by Ilis, euphoric with the emotions of being free in the air, with the wind and the light that crossed through his essence.

Obolil stopped. *And now?*

It's the barrier! It feels like a giant invisible wall is in front of us!

Very good. You're less dumb than I thought you were. That

41

charlatan of a wizard thought the barrier was no longer here. Poor idiot! If he were at least as talented as a court jester, he would have realized that it hadn't disappeared, it had only shifted. He stayed silent for a few seconds, lost in his own thoughts. *But this is a good sign, because it means that whoever is still keeping it alive is not strong enough to push it very far North. Ilis, under no circumstances must you ever try to travel further South than this point here, or the barrier will decimate your spirit.*

But after the last ritual, Aldin swore that he had succeeded! He said he had even travelled down to the Southern lands.

Aldin was a fool. He probably didn't even manage to travel through the astral planes. Back when I was around he was never able to, and I doubt he was able to learn by himself after I was gone. He probably only imagined that he had. Simple self-delusion. Besides, if he never taught you how to do it, it's probably because he couldn't do it himself.

So is that why he died on that ship? Did he think he had eliminated the barrier and travelled to the Southern lands, when in reality, he hadn't?

The thought made Ilis shiver. He remembered how proud his first master had been when he had announced that he was able to do what no wizard at any point in time had ever been able to do. But Ilis felt his heart ache for the fate of the poor boys who had left on those ships. The best soldiers and finest sailors in the kingdom had been chosen, and they were given the honor of sailing on the first ship that, after so much time, would take off to seek new lands and meet new people. Some of those boys had even been his friends.

Concentrate, boy! Even if we can't move beyond this barrier, we can still detect the presence of the energies on the island from here. Don't imagine you're on the island, or else you won't make it out of this alive. Instead, try to feel the energies, even the most subtle ones.

Ilis had no idea how to create such a connection to the island. He knew very little about these kinds of magic; Aldin himself had only understood a few basic notions. But he was certain that at least part of the ritual the deceased wizard had performed was successful. He could feel the movement of the material and, right after, the blood, the dismay, the shouts, the screams, the confusion...and the death.

Obolil's shadow in front of him started to waver. He reached a level of transparence at which he was indistinguishable from the

42

surrounding air. Then, suddenly, he became denser once again.

Hmm. I see you've stayed behind to wander through your useless thoughts. Learn how to concentrate, because we need to come back often if we want to learn something more about our enemy.

Our enemy? They're not all dead?

The island seems to be deserted. I guess Aldin wasn't a total failure after all. But although it's well concealed, the energy of the Temple remains strong. And that's what emanates the protections that keep the barrier active. Not even I can perceive what hides inside of it, but if the Temple is able to diffuse such strong energy, there must certainly be somebody in there.

So what can we do now, master?

We can wait for them to leave. They can't stay hiding in there like little mice forever. But for now, let's go back. Show me if you've learned how to move through the astral planes, boy.

Ilis visualized the laboratory they had left. He felt himself being sucked back down and a few seconds later returned, next to his own body. The transparent, ethereal image of Obolil appeared at his side. Yet again, he couldn't help noticing how different it was from the crumpled up creature flopping over the table down below.

In the astral planes, we project the image that we feel of ourselves. If you think you're a white bear, that's what you'll appear as. But now we have other matters to attend to. Do you know how to go back to your body?

No, master. I've never tried before.

That dimwit should have at least taught you the rudimentary theoretical elements.

Such criticism made Ilis feel rather uneasy. He wished he could perform some magic action that would impress the wizard, but he guessed that no matter what he did, he wouldn't receive anything but criticism. For the moment, he decided it was better to resign himself to that.

15

2000 years earlier

Moltil, Brunus and Zalbia ran breathlessly along the wall of the palace perpendicular to the sea. The three children had no idea where to hide. The soldiers had left their flying ships and were now everywhere. Below them, a cluster of foot soldiers appeared in the courtyard. They were wounded. Some of them struggled to stay on their feet. They looked for a way out but, before they could take another step, two enemies appeared at the end of the courtyard. They moved forward calmly, unhurried.

One of the soldiers encouraged his comrades: "For the Kingdom of Isk! For our king! For our homeland!" The soldiers pounced upon the two coming towards them, who placidly lifted their fingers and, with a single gesture, emitted a beam of light which, in a flash, dematerialized their assailants.

Terrified, the children watched the scene unfold as they tried to remain hidden. Zalbia, however, couldn't contain a moan of horror and disgust. Moltil quickly covered her mouth with his hand and held her close to him.

One of the two enemies looked up in their direction, but luckily didn't see them; they were shielded by the barriers of the walkway.

"Hunter to ship. The courtyard is clear. How many are left in the palace?" one of the two asked, directing his question downwards.

Moltil looked out, spying on them. They were standing straight, looking around in their purple uniforms. The one that had spoken wasn't holding any sort of communication device.

"Another thirty-five," his partner said, "hiding in the kitchens, in the dungeons, the tunnels underneath the palace and in the rooms of the upper wing. And there's still another ninety-eight outside. Let's go, the earlier we finish, the quicker we can go home." The two swiftly left the courtyard.

Moltil motioned for Brunus and Zalbia to keep quiet and follow him. The three children slunk along the wall and into a guard tower. Before going back in, Zalbia glanced out at their flying ships, anchored a few hundred yards from the coast and a few dozen feet above the surface of the water. They shone in the sun, grey with a large, upside-down purple V on their sides.

Once in the tower, Moltil headed down the spiral staircase. Zalbia tugged at his arm: "Where are you going?" she asked in a whisper.

"We need to get out of here. They're crawling through the palace," the boy responded.

"But didn't you hear what they said? There are still a lot outside who they want to eliminate. They're practically done here. If we stay inside, they won't find us, maybe we'll survive."

"But Zalbia, my father's armies are outside. If we join together with them, we'll be able to fight them."

"Moltil! Can't you see what they have? All they need to do is raise a finger and whatever's in front of them disintegrates. How can the soldiers fight against that?"

Moltil felt defeated: "Zalbia, we have to try. My father raised me to be a king. I can't hide like a little flea!"

"No, no, don't go. Please. Don't do it!" Brunus interjected. Moltil and Zalbia turned to look at him. Zalbia's little brother was a few years younger than them. His lips trembled as his spoke, his face dripping with sweat, since all of that running was just too much for his chubby body. "You s-saw what they're capable of. If they see us, we'll all d-die."

"Brunus, they're my people. These are my subjects, who I will rule over. This is why I was born. You two don't have to come with me if you don't want to. You can just stay here and hide."

Zalbia raised her voice a little more than she intended to: "Moltil, you're setting yourself up for suicide! Can't you see? The only ones who are going to survive are those who can stay hidden! Look at their astroships! Look at their weapons! If your father and mother and brothers are dead and you throw yourself towards death, then who will be left to govern the survivors?"

Moltil bit his lip. They had started running after the screams from the palace had awoken them in the middle of the night. They had used tunnels, secret doors and all kinds of hiding places. Every time, as soon as those calm and incessant footsteps came closer, they had run away.

Brunus shook him out of his thoughts: "M-maybe they don't want to eliminate us."

Moltil and Zalbia turned to look at him, questioningly.

"They p-passed right by us already so many times...it seems as if they're ignoring us. M-maybe they only want to k-kill the g-grownups."

Moltil wanted to answer but Zalbia beat him to it: "He's right. That's why we're still alive. They're not looking for us. They don't want us."

"But..." Moltil began before the sound of footsteps at the bottom of the staircase stopped him cold.

Zalbia headed towards the door to their right, which opened into a long corridor.

Brunus followed her and, reluctantly, Moltil. The three children ran down the wide hallway flooded with sunlight. To their left, through a giant glass window, they could see the three flying ships, immobile and menacing. To their right, splendid tapestries depicted the ancient rulers of the kingdom.

Halfway down the hallway, a door just in front of them stood wide open.

Zalbia instinctively opened another door hidden behind the luxurious tapestry. It led to a tiny room used as a storage space, where the servants stacked chairs whenever royal balls were held in the main hall.

The three children got in and shut the door, standing in the darkness.

"Shh..." Zalbia whispered. Only the incessant chattering of Brunus' teeth could be heard.

"Calm down, little brother," his sister whispered in his ear.

Moltil was standing to her right, frozen. She took his hand in hers, sincerely hoping the young prince wouldn't try to do anything rash.

The sound of footsteps rang outside the door, then stopped near them.

What, are they admiring the tapestries? Zalbia wondered.

"What do you think, should we kill them?" asked a man's voice.

"Orders are orders. We're only doing our job," responded a woman's voice, drily.

"Of course, but still, we've had relations with these people for thousands of years. That sort of punishment seems a little excessive to me, don't you think?"

"They didn't respect the treaty. They did what they wanted without consulting anyone else. They're the ones responsible for this river of innocent blood."

"I know, but if we keep going on like this, we won't have any more allies around here."

"It's just as well. The only thing we get from the North are headaches. Come on, let's go. If you really like these tapestries so much, we can send a squad to collect them for you later."

The footsteps resumed, coming closer to the door and then moving onwards.

Zalbia let out a sigh of relief; she could feel Brunus was about to explode.

"Wait, I'm getting a signal from the ship," the woman said.

"Where?"

"There." she indicated.

The steps came back to the hiding place. Brunus started to whimper.

"No," his sister whispered in his ear. "Please, not now."

The steps stopped in front of the door.

"How do you open this thing?" the man asked.

A few seconds of silence.

"Step aside," she said. The door disappeared and the room was bathed in light. Zalbia instinctively looked over at Multil, sure her friend would jump on the two invaders. But the boy was frozen, terrorized, his eyes wild.

"Again?" the woman exclaimed. Then she added, as if she were talking to an invisible being in front of them: "It's the same three kids as before. Please deactivate these three signals or we'll never get done here."

Incredulous, Zalbia watched the man and woman leave their field of vision.

16

Lil looked at her husband's peaceful face. Contrary to her expectations, Bashinoir still hadn't woken up. Miril and Lil had discussed leaving the Temple. Neither could go out for an extended period of time, and Lil finally understood why. But she didn't want to venture out by herself either, although there were animals to look after and winter crops to harvest. Their survival depended on those types of tasks. She also wanted to see what had happened to her old home. But she couldn't bring herself to go alone.

Lil had spent the past few days taking care of a few minor chores around the Temple, tidying up the kitchen and some of the rooms.

Meanwhile, Miril had spent most of her time in the rooms tucked away deep within the building's depths. Whenever their paths crossed, the priestess would force herself to exchange a few friendly words, yet it was obvious she was exhausted. Lil wondered how Miril could survive while bearing a burden which, until just a few days earlier, had been shared between her and the priest.

Lil felt very much alone.

Is this how it's going to be from now on? There were only three of them left and, just to survive, they'd have to work very hard. Bashinoir would need to do things it normally took dozens of men to do. Miril would have her hands full with the magic rites necessary for their protection. As for Lil, well...she wasn't really sure what would be required of her.

Looking at Bashinoir's placid expression, Lil suddenly felt a pang of guilt. Had she been a good wife? Yes, it was true, she had purposely done a few things to inspire his jealousy now and again, but deep down she had always loved him with all of her heart, and their marriage had, until that fateful day, been content and fulfilling. A few months earlier she and her husband had actually started discussing the idea of children. Bashinoir's eyes shone whenever he talked about expanding the family, and for Lil, becoming a mother would mean achieving one of her biggest dreams.

But now the life of a priestess awaited her. How could she explain this to him? And how would he take it? A few days earlier, almost everything they had lived for had tragically disappeared in front of their eyes, and now, all that he had left – his wife – would also be taken away from him.

"Lil, I'm sorry I couldn't join you for dinner. I had to rebalance the energies, they've decreased far too much over the last few days. But now everything's back to normal."

Those sorts of matters still sounded foreign to Lil. Yet Miril talked about them naturally, as if she were referring to things both of them knew.

Lil had prepared dinner for both of them, and even though Miril was late, she had decided to wait for her before eating.

"Lil, have you had a chance to think about what I asked you?"

Actually, I haven't thought about anything but that. "Yes, Miril." she answered, hesitant.

"So what do you think?" Miril urged in a serious tone of voice.

Lil looked at her, surprised. She had never been asked to express her own opinion regarding big decisions. She wanted to explain her thoughts to Miril, but she couldn't find the right words.

"Lil, you're an adult. The initiation process isn't the same as it is for newborns. For a baby, it's purely spontaneous: a child who starts down this path of consciousness picks everything up quite naturally. There will probably be very heavy resistance coming from inside of you. In any case, the most important thing is that you're convinced you want to do it. Even though it may seem like something you absolutely *have* to do, unless you're fully committed, it'll be impossible to go forward, and we won't be able to bring you to the level you need to reach in order to do what's necessary. Take some more time to think about it, Lil. We can only begin when you really want to start."

Inside her own mind, Lil reacted strongly to Miril's words. Feeling obligated had made everything seem simple: she would have preferred to tell her husband that, for the good of the island and the preservation of its magical protections, she had to become a priestess. How could she tell him that it was *also* her choice? What words could she use to explain that? *There are only three of us left and I decided to leave you to become a priestess* – or *Sorry, I know you've lost everyone you ever loved and every dream you ever had in life, but I've recently decided to spend my future serving the gods.*

No, she didn't want the opportunity to choose. If this was going to happen, it would happen because it's what the priestess and the elders wanted, in order to maintain the magical protections that shielded the island from the evil forces that had been lurking in the shadows for centuries. Forces which, at least as far as she could tell, had finally found a little crack they could slip through. No, she needed to feel obligated.

"Miril, I'll do what I have to do. If I need to become a priestess for the good of the island, if that is my destiny, if that is what you're asking me to do, if that is what the gods want from me, then I'll do it," Lil stated, delivering her words all in one breath as she feared that, once she paused, she wouldn't have the courage to continue.

A moan came from behind the two women. They turned around, fearing that Bashinoir had suddenly taken a turn for the worse. Eyes wide open, he returned their gaze. His face was full of bewilderment, pain, and resignation.

Miril calmly looked back at him. Lil felt her heart ache. *How long has he been awake for? Did he hear everything? Does he already know? My husband...my lover, my sweet, strong, brave, darling husband.*

She didn't want to cry, but she couldn't hold the tears back from streaming down her face.

Bashinoir wanted to move closer to her. He tried to get up, but was still too weak. The priestess Miril went to examine his wound.

17

Tuirl entered the large bathroom. The humidity smothered his face and, for a moment, he had trouble breathing. "A-*hem*," he cleared his throat, trying to announce his presence indirectly.

"What do you want now?" King Beanor brusquely barked.

The room was circular. Tall columns lined half of its perimeter, and from the other side, steam curled up from the hot water of a gigantic pool.

Two of the king's wives laid comfortably on the side of the pool, at the mercy of the royal masseurs. In the water, lying next to the king, another two wives rubbed their hands, lips, and tongues all over the monarch's body. Beanor shook his leg and a fifth girl emerged from the water right in front of him.

Tuirl turned around, embarrassed.

"Say something, why don't you! What do you want to bother me with now?"

The father did nothing but tend to royal affairs, day and night. But his son just hops from one orgy to another! Tuirl bitterly reflected.

The young lady to Beanor's right moved her tongue along his neck all the way to his earlobe, which she began to nibble. The other woman submerged in the water began playing with the curly locks of his hairy chest.

"Stop, stop. Don't you see I have more important things to do now?" the king protested, roughly shoving them away.

Ignoring what he just said, the women went right back to what they had been doing. They weren't going to waste a chance to win the favors of their husband and king. There were plenty of wives, and it wasn't every day that each had her turn to be with him.

Doling out a few slaps, the king wriggled free and made his way up the stairs, leaving the water. The wives looked disappointed. If their time had been interrupted so soon, they probably wouldn't get any little gifts. The youngest, who had the fewest jewels and wanted them much more badly than her older colleagues, tried everything she could to pounce upon the partially erect member of the king, who merely stepped aside.

"Come on, advisor. Start talking before these mewling cats attack me."

Proud of his virility, Beanor moved towards Tuirl, who was trying to decide where he should direct his gaze.

"You asked me to immediately report any news from the magical experiments."

"Right. So?"

"The wizard Obolil told me that he and the apprentice were able to assess the situation on the island. It actually appears as if no one remains living on the surface."

"All dead, all dead. Finally, we've exterminated them!" Beanor triumphantly interrupted him. "Those worms! It took two thousand years, but we did it! And it was Beanor who succeeded in accomplishing what all of his forefathers had failed to do!"

Tuirl doubted that the credit would be attributed to the king in the long run, but decided it would be wiser to drop the matter.

"So why is the barrier still there?" Beanor suddenly asked, realizing that something didn't add up.

"If you will allow me to continue, I was actually going to tell you that, in fact, the Temple is still emitting strong energies."

"What does that mean? Get to the point before I cut off your head and throw the rest of your body down the toilet." The excitement of a few seconds ago had disappeared. Beanor would be glad to unleash his anger upon the imbecile standing before him.

"It means, your Majesty, that someone may indeed remain inside of the Temple – meaning someone must have escaped the massacre orchestrated by Aldin."

"Someone in the Temple? Who?"

"Unfortunately, Obolil and Ilis weren't able to answer that question. As you know, even in the astral dimension, we are unable to overcome that barrier. And the energies of the Temple blocked every attempt to investigate its interior."

"So we need to wait for those little rodents to come out, then."

"That's precisely what Obolil recommended."

"Then we need to make sure that, whenever they do leave, one of our two wizards is waiting for them."

"Your Majesty, it will probably take some time."

"Tuirl! Have you lost your mind?" Beanor interjected. His temper flaring, he approached the advisor with his fists raised.

Instinctively, Tuirl took a few steps back, pressing his back against a column.

"They'll take turns, one at night, one at day. One of them must always have their eyes glued on that goddamn island."

"But your Majesty, you know that such abuse of astral travel would entail serious risks for the health of the wizards. It would also consume their vital energies. It's hard to say what the consequences would be."

"The sooner the barrier comes down, the sooner we'll enjoy the benefits. We've been trying to end our isolation for two thousand years. I'm not waiting any longer. Send the guards out to make sure the wizards do what I just said they should do."

"Your Majesty, that may be counterproductive."

"Are you questioning my orders?" Beanor asked in a threatening tone, moving towards Tuirl. The advisor braced himself against the column. Beanor leaned in, breathing just a few inches away from the advisor's face.

"No, of course not. I'll immediately arrange for the guards to take their positions," the elderly man whispered in a tiny voice.

18

Bashinoir couldn't sleep. Lil and Miril had spent a lot of time taking care of him. He had cooperated as they washed him, dressed him in clean clothes, changed his bandages, and tended to the wounds all over his body.

His wife had remained silent, probably embarrassed by what he had overheard them talking about, when they thought he was still sleeping.

The priestess had seemed as calm as usual. After a little while, they had urged him to get some rest.

His wife, a priestess! For the good of the island! Bashinoir could hardly believe it, and he understood what that meant. No part of his former life had gone unchanged; none of the little pleasures that used to warm his heart, in spite of the difficult circumstances of everyday life, remained. And now he would have to lose her: Lil.

When they had taken refuge in the Temple after the dramatic events that had exterminated almost the entire population, although there were only three of them left, he had assumed that at least he and Lil could still have children. One way or another, they or their descendents would have found a way to survive and maybe even leave the island.

He never would have imagined that, by such a strange twist of fate, he wouldn't have any descendents, that he and Lil wouldn't have any babies. They had survived. Really, *they* had survived. Wasn't that a sign from the gods?

Unfortunately, that doesn't seem to be the case.

Why had they waited for so long? They had everything they needed. Bashinoir and Lil owned a house, though it was just a single room built around a hearth. Yet they had both assumed that, before having children, they would build a bigger and better place with more rooms. He had gone to build the new structure every day after he finished work, before the sun went down. Together, they had gone looking for the new location where they were going to live. When, excited, they had found the cliff with the breathtaking view, they knew they had found it: that would be where they would welcome their family into this world. The village was just a 5-minute walk away, and there was a tidy little path that led down to the seashore, where they could go fishing.

Everything was almost ready. An elder had even advised him that the ideal time to conceive their first child would be right after the new moon.

But then those horrendous rock shards had hammered down upon his people. His marriage was over, and Lil would never give him any children.

For the good of the island.

He knew there had always been more than one priest, but he had never wondered why. Before allowing his wife to leave him forever, he wanted to at least ask her why. He wouldn't object, he wouldn't try to stop her, that was for sure. One never questioned orders from the priestess. But when it came to his wife and her decisions, he felt he was almost entitled to a more detailed explanation.

The priestess seemed so nice when she spoke to Lil. Bashinoir hoped that she would be equally open and communicative with him.

He no longer had the strength to stay awake. He fell into an anxious, restless sleep.

19

Lying in bed, Beanor observed the perfect body of the woman stretched out, nude, alongside him. He had just taken her savagely, and now he was hungry. The girl picked up a tray overflowing with berries and handed him one.

Beanor's eyes lingered on her breasts: they weren't very large, but they had an imperious bearing to them which drove him crazy. Added to her dark complexion and incredibly green eyes, she was quite the rare pearl in the kingdom. Since he had chosen her for a concubine, he had preferred to keep her in his bed more than any of the others.

"My Lord, may I come in?"

"Aleia?" Beanor exclaimed, surprised.

The woman entered. She was tall, with her auburn hair swept back. Her body was dressed in a red tunic trimmed with gold.

"What can I do for you, darling?"

The girl lying in bed was surprised: it was rare to hear the king speak so gently to someone. Embarrassed, she pulled the sheet up over her body, though it wasn't the first time Aleia had ever seen her naked.

"I want to talk to you." Aleia announced, heading towards the bed.

She's still a beautiful woman, Beanor reflected. *It's been a while since I've ridden her, but it'd be strange to do it with a woman that...old. Though I have to admit she still has something about her. Maybe one of these nights, who knows.* Subjugating her would also help her to remember her place: he had heard rumors that, among the concubines, she acted like a queen and forced the others to cater to her desires and serve her needs.

Aleia patiently waited for the king's focus to move from her body back to her face.

"I'd like to talk to you. In private, if that's at all possible."

Beanor shot her a dirty look. He wanted to respond rudely, but instead turned to the girl: "I don't want you getting cold, so stay here in bed like a good girl. If you repeat a word of what you're going to hear, I'll cut your head off. Understand? Now give me some of that wine."

The girl, humiliated by the threat, reached for the chalice of wine on the bedside table and handed it to him.

"Come here, Aleia. Have a seat on the bed."

Beanor moved over to make room for Aleia, pushing away the concubine, who didn't protest. As his first wife sat down on the edge, he passed a hand over her rear end, thrilled that the flesh was still firm.

Aleia waited. When Beanor finished his inspection, the woman went straight to the point: "My Lord, I know what you've asked your advisor to do. He went down to the prison to request the services of old Obolil, who now, together with the apprentice, is again hard at work looking for a solution to the barrier."

Beanor looked at her, astonished. Then, in a sarcastic tone of voice, he started teasing her: "Well, well, well. You know so much, don't you? I thought you only worried about the pussies of your little girlfriends."

"Your Majesty," she exclaimed, her pride wounded. "You would be surprised to hear of all the duties that have fallen under my responsibility. Who do you think looks after the royal palace while you're busy with other things?"

"Now, now. Don't get upset. I know you take care of a lot, and I'm happy to entrust you with such responsibility, considering how diligently you perform your duties. But tell me: why are you interested in these affairs?"

"Because, your Majesty, I'm not so sure it's the right thing to do!"

Beanor looked at her, intrigued, as if he only now saw her for the first time.

"Listen," she continued. "We've already had two failures under the orders of the advisor. Do you think that's merely a coincidence? But now there's another, more important question. The advisor came up with the idea to put the old wizard back to work, the same one who already failed. Why did you go along with such an idea?"

Beanor didn't like it when people implied things through their words. "What are you trying to say? Say what you mean!" he yelled, raising his hand as if he was going to slap her.

"Your Majesty, I'm being very clear! I think that Tuirl is giving you bad advice, because he actually doesn't want the barrier to be broken!"

A few seconds later, Beanor burst out into raucous laughter.

"Women! Sometimes I wonder if they have any brains at all. Give me your hand," he ordered her, but instead of waiting, took it himself and placed it on his penis.

"I remember that you used to be very good at these sorts of things..."

"But -" she objected.

"Do you dare refuse your spouse and king?"

"Of course not," she replied, aware that nobody within those walls was immune to the king's rage.

"Very well. So just use one hand, like how you used to. I'll give you an evening all to yourself, if you're good, and then we can play with our mouths and all the rest."

Resigned, Aleia started to move her hand down slowly, gently squeezing his penis.

Beanor leaned against the pillow and closed his eyes.

"Oh..." he let out. *Yes, that's it...that's exactly what I remember.*

Aleia continued her slow strokes. Beanor, panting with pleasure, licked his lips. "Uhhh..." he groaned. He grabbed the girl with his arm. "You, come stand over me. I want to have a little taste of you. But turn around. I want you to watch my first wife. You need to learn how to do the same thing."

Thoroughly annoyed, the young concubine obeyed and pointed her rump towards him. He started first by breathing in her sex, then forcefully grabbed her hips, pulled her to him and penetrated her with his tongue.

20

Bashinoir rubbed his face, opening his eyes. It had been a restless, dreamless night. Still low on energy, he had tried, not without difficulty, to sit up. Once his feet were on the floor, he struggled to stand up on his own. His head immediately started to spin but, keeping one hand on the bed, he was able to pull himself upright and took a few cautious steps, moving as far as the fireplace.

When Lil came into the room, she was surprised to see him standing up. Her heart beating wildly, she ran towards him and, without saying a word, threw her arms around his neck. Both felt the urge to kiss one another but stopped, then backed off, keeping an arm's length of distance between them.

But Bashinoir didn't want to hold back. *She's my wife!* He lifted her chin with one hand and their lips united in a deep, intense kiss. Lil didn't want that moment to end: her desire for that contact had been burning for far too long.

"Good morning, Bashinoir. I see you're doing much better," Miril greeted him as she came into the room. She appeared peaceful, even tired. The scene did not seem to disturb her, but Bashinoir and Lil still felt guilty for being caught in such an intimate embrace.

"How about we all have some breakfast together?" Miril suggested.

Lil sighed. She already knew what the priestess wanted to talk about over their meal. However, once they were sitting around the table, the priestess instead started discussing more practical things.

"Alone on this island, we need to make a few changes if we want to survive. It would probably be best to build new stables for the livestock, closer to the Temple."

Bashinoir and Lil listened, stunned, to what Miril had to say. They never would have imagined that a priestess would pay any attention to such basic, pragmatic things.

Miril continued: "It's a practical consideration, sure, but it also has to do with magic. I think that at this point, it would be best to create an area around us over which we can extend the protections of the Temple, which are the most powerful protections we have."

Bashinoir had many questions he wanted to ask her, but he didn't feel comfortable talking to the priestess. She, however, had perceived his desire and encouraged him: "Please, Bashinoir. Ask me what you want to know."

The man felt as if she had read his thoughts.

"Do you mean to say an area where those...rock shards can't fall on us?"

"Exactly, Bashinoir. The protections that have, until recently, covered the island may no longer be enough. Or they may have simply been overcome by the magical powers of our enemy. But I do know that the protections of the Temple are strong enough to resist any attack and hide us from everyone's sight."

"But why can't we protect the entire island?" Lil objected. Her husband looked at her, stunned. How dare his wife address the priestess so rudely?

"I'm sorry, but I'm afraid it's not possible, at least not now. The rituals would become so complex that it would require the assistance of several priests. And...there aren't very many of us."

Lil and Bashinoir understood that the conversation had reached the point both of them wanted to avoid.

Bashinoir tried to be brave. "Priestess, if it's necessary for Lil to take on the duties of a priestess, I'll be happy to take care of all the practical tasks myself. I'll start moving the animals as soon as I can."

Miril smiled: "I'm sorry, Bashinoir. Believe me. The magical protections around us require the support of at least two priests, who take turns and also work together on the main rituals. The initiation phase will be very hard for Lil, as well as tiring for me. As long as she remains a novice, I'll do my best to carry on the rites myself. But I have to be honest with you: I won't be able to last for very long."

Upon hearing those words, Bashinoir realized how Miril, speaking so calmly and naturally, looked as if she were being crushed by a heavy weight. It was just dawn, and yet her face was worn, as if she had stayed awake the entire night. *We need to help her any way we can.*

The priestess smiled kindly: "If you agree, we can rearrange the living quarters to accommodate all of us. I'll stay where I've always been. Lil will have the novice's quarters and you, Bashinoir, can stay in the guest rooms. The area for priests is more comfortable and better heated, but the energy level of those spaces is not suitable for someone who hasn't taken the oaths and right now I don't have the resources to make the necessary adjustments. When we get a chance to perform that type of ritual, you can move. We can take a look at your new quarters now, if you'd like."

We've finally found a bigger house, Bashinoir thought, watching his wife get up to clear the table. *But at what cost?*

21

Tuirl removed a large key from his pocket and pushed open the heavy door, revealing a long sequence of stairs spiraling down into the darkness. For the thousandth time, he looked around, furtively. He had taken every precaution to make sure nobody saw him, yet he felt a gnawing sense of anxiety whenever he went down to that place.

The torchlight illuminated the stairs, which appeared to trail on into infinity. As he walked down, the temperature gradually dropped. Spiders and flies crawled about everywhere. Tuirl stared at the wall to his right, searching for a stone with a slightly rosy hue.

When he finally found it, he counted down another twelve stairs, then bent down to push the third stone from the ground. Nothing happened. *Did I count wrong?* After a few seconds, part of the wall started moving back, creating just enough space for a man to walk through. Tuirl entered and, pressing a stone to his right, activated the mechanism to close the wall behind him.

Using the flame from his torch, he lit the lamps hanging from the walls and studied the room. It was exactly how he remembered leaving it. On either side there were dusty bookcases full of scrolls and ancient-looking volumes. A faldstool stood in the middle of the room, with a stone basin full of black liquid in front of it. Every once in a while, a drop fell from the ceiling straight into the bowl. The liquid overflowed, dripping down the side opposite the entry door. There were no partitions in this room, just empty space and, hanging below the ceiling, a thick layer of fog. The liquid dripped down into the abyss. Tuirl looked around yet again, full of an unjustified disquiet. *Nobody knows this room exists. No curious eye has ever seen what lies behind these walls.*

He knelt down, took a deep breath and held his hands over the black liquid.

She's going to be very, very angry.

He had done all he possibly could to keep postponing their meeting, but he knew he'd eventually have to explain things to her, and now he couldn't buy any more time. For a few seconds, he thought maybe he should turn back and run away. He could come back the week after next, justifying his repeated absences with court engagements and his duties as advisor. *No, if I keep putting her off, I could end up with some unpleasant consequences.*

Resigned, he dipped his hands into the liquid.

Kneeling down in front of the altar, Miril immediately sensed the contact. She rose to her feet and headed towards the inner chambers of the Temple. She entered a small, square room, closing the door behind her. *Lil would never come to this area of the Temple, and Bashinoir isn't even allowed here, but it's better not to run any risks.*

She placed her hands in the black liquid of the rocky hollow and immediately the image of Tuirl materialized in front of her, first faint, then growing more clearly defined.

"Why did you wait so long to contact me?" she reproached him drily.

"Priestess, I humbly ask for your forgiveness, but my engagements at court did not allow me to come here earlier."

"Engagements at court, or fear of facing me?"

Tuirl felt an icy chill travel down his spine. As he had expected, the priestess was incredibly angry with him. How could it have been otherwise? The advisor understood punishment was in order, and that, this time, it would be very harsh.

"Priestess Miril, I understand what happened cannot be justified -"

"The entire population of the island has been exterminated. *My people.* Do you understand what that means?"

"Yes, priestess. I'm aware of the situation, and I still don't understand how the old wizard Aldin was able to pull off such an extensive magical operation. He always seemed to be completely incompetent, and I never failed to perform the acts of sabotage you ordered me to."

"So what happened, then?" Miril was barely able to contain her rage. Tuirl had never even heard her raise her voice before.

"I...I don't know. Aldin may have worked secretly on a few spells, without my knowing."

"How could that possibly have gotten by you? I ordered you to go through that laboratory every single night! You had very precise instructions. You were to report to me, in advance, on any spell Aldin was preparing to cast."

"Priestess, believe me, that's what I always did. I never kept any information from you."

"And yet, you were so careless as to let the preparations for a spell – a spell that exterminated an entire people – get right past you!"

Miril was beside herself with anger. Tuirl started to fear for his own life.

"Tuirl," she began again. "The preparations for a spell of that magnitude require years, if not decades. Are you sure you never noticed anything?"

"Priestess Miril, please, believe me. I reported every ritual, spell, and magical action that the wizard Aldin undertook, directly to you. You had information on the progress of every spell he cast to break down the barrier and, as a matter of fact, following your orders, I was able to alter the composition of the elements, without raising any suspicion. He was so sure of his success that he decided to set sail on the same ship, taking on someone else's appearance. And when the ship crashed, he died along with the rest."

Aldin is dead? The priestess, who had been deprived of this precious contact with Tuirl for weeks, wasn't aware of that particular detail.

"So, the court wizard is no longer alive?"

"Precisely, priestess. And, if you'll allow me to continue, it's also partly because of me."

For once he followed the instructions properly. "So what has the king decided to do now? Will he give up on these designs?"

"Actually, if you want to know the truth, upon my counsel, he decided to call old Obolil back into service."

"And what made you suggest such a thing to him?"

"I don't trust the apprentice, young Ilis. We don't know what he's capable of. I thought if the king gave him the time and resources to go ahead with his own experiments, maybe he would have learned something that would prove to be dangerous for us. But, on the other hand, if he's under the guidance of the wizard Obolil, then there's no way anything is going to change. As you know full well, Obolil never had any talent to him. Besides, he's exhausted, after spending twenty years locked up in a cell, kept company by his own excrement. His memory is weak and he's full of hatred for the king. In other words, under Obolil's guidance, we can be sure that Ilis isn't going to get very far with his studies."

Though Miril understood the logic behind Tuirl's plan, she knew he was prone to making major errors of judgment.

"So you went ahead and set all of that up without asking for my approval?"

Her menacing tone of voice washed away the tiny bits of confidence Tuirl had managed to recover. "Priestess, please, forgive me. I was afraid that King Beanor would act upon his own initiative. You know better than I do that the monarch is so proud that he'd never back out of a decision made by his own volition. I had to improvise."

"Tuirl, you are a follower of the Goddess. I am her manifestation in this world. She will not grant you permission to make any more mistakes, for any reason whatsoever. If your lack of obedience creates any further problems, you'll pay with your life." *But not now, because you're the only spy I have.*

"I understand, priestess. I know I shouldn't have done what I did and I humbly ask you to forgive me. The weight of my responsibilities keeps me awake at night. Your people have lost their lives. But tell me, please, to alleviate my grief and guilt, even just a little – were any of them spared? Did anyone survive on the island along with you? I can't bear to think you've been condemned to solitude."

"Don't you worry about me. And it's none of your business whether or not any people of the island have survived. The only thing you need to worry about from now on is coming here at least once a week and telling me everything that happens inside of that palace. I want to know about every move Obolil makes. Now go."

"Priestess, I humbly ask for your forgiveness."

"The Goddess does not pardon incompetence."

Miril lifted her hands out of the black liquid. In the secret room, hidden within the foundation of the royal palace, her figure vanished. The fog turned grey and became denser in front of Tuirl's eyes, now full of relief.

65

22

King Beanor sat at the table. His sole reason for dining was to enjoy the show he had arranged for himself.

A few days earlier, walking around the perimeter of the palace, he had noticed the gorgeous shape of a young maiden moving through the hovels down below. Immediately infatuated, he had sent the royal guards to go fetch her.

Upon his orders, the maiden was entrusted to his other wives, so she could be properly trained. A few hours later, however, Beanor had decided he could no longer wait, ignoring Aleia's protests, who tried to convince him that the girl was not ready.

Watching her, the king decided that she did indeed need more preparation before she could truly be called a dancer. Yet this was a minor detail the king was happy to overlook for the time being.

With a wave of his hand, still clinging onto a chicken leg, he motioned for the musicians to stop.

"Come here!" he ordered the young woman, as he continued chewing with gusto.

Cautious and a bit intimidated, the girl obeyed. When she was close to the monarch, he calmly placed a hand on her hip and roughly spun her around.

"Hmm..." he lowed. "Put your hands on the table and bend over!" He carefully scrutinized her rear end, prodding it methodically.

"Interesting. Young, firm, perfect in every aspect." Beanor was thoroughly enchanted by the perfect rotundity of her gluteals. He caressed them and pawed at them for several moments, then slipped his hand between her thighs, moving until he could feel her sex.

"They promised me you were a virgin. Stay that way and one of these nights we'll have a little fun, just you and me."

He explored her vulva with a finger. "Just look how tight you are! Not bad...not bad at all!" He brought his finger to his nose. "What a lovely smell...Guards!" he shouted.

The young woman tried to stand back up but, with a hand on her back, he forced her to remain bent over. "Call the advisor over here."

One guard left the room and came back a few moments later with Tuirl, who found King Beanor intent upon his examination.

"Advisor, look at this ass. What do you see?"

The elderly man quietly came forward to get a better look. "Your majesty, this young lady appears to be quite lovely. And I believe she would make an excellent addition, if that's what you wanted to know."

"Yes, yes, of course. But take a good look. Bend down, if your eyes are too weak."

Doing his best to hide his annoyance, Tuirl obeyed.

"Your majesty, it appears to me as if her physique is *extremely* lovely."

Slapping the woman's behind, Beanor exclaimed: "It's small! Don't you see? Don't you understand? It's a young and compact ass, just how I like them. How is it possible that all of my wives enter the palace with asses like this and then let themselves go?"

"Your Majesty, I believe that...the abundance and variety of food you provide your wives helps them to take on more...generous proportions. But I can assure you that, in my opinion, all of your companions have retained their charms."

Do I have to order them to eat less? Beanor wondered. *Then would they be...less energetic in bed?* "Fine, right. I don't know why I bother asking you these things. I've never seen you go around with anything attractive on your arm!"

Tuirl refrained from commenting.

Noticing the advisor's uneasiness, Beanor decided to continue with his rant.

"I've heard what people are saying around the palace. Some think you're plotting something behind my back! What do you have to say about that?"

Tuirl turned pale. *He can't possibly know about me going down to the secret room. Nobody saw me, nobody knows.*

"I see you've turned pale now," the king provoked him.

"Your Majesty. You know I could never have anything to do with such a crime. I've served you faithfully for many years, and before you, I served your father. If such rumors do indeed persist, I would appreciate it if you could tell me who they're coming from, so that I can take the appropriate measures to set the record straight."

King Beanor seemed thoughtful. With one hand, he continued prodding the rump that remained, immobile, in front of him, and with the other hand, he grabbed some meat from a platter. Biting into a lamb chop, he let his intelligence shine forth from his mouth,

67

still full: "Your reaction is hardly convincing. I wonder if these voices are actually telling the truth, then?"

He only said that to provoke me, and I fell like a fool into his trap.

Tuirl replied in a firm and resolute manner: "Your Majesty, there is absolutely no reason and no way I could possibly plot anything without you knowing about it."

Beanor remained unconvinced.

"And, with regards to your first question, perhaps it would be best to no longer deprive yourself of the pleasure this young lady arouses in you," Tuirl continued.

Beanor's attention immediately returned to the rump which, during the discussion, he had continued to poke and prod.

"Don't tempt me, advisor. You know that even the king has to respect tradition. Until I take her as my wife, I can't...help myself."

"Well, why don't we officiate the wedding now?"

Beanor froze, holding the lamb chop in mid-air. "Officiate the wedding? Now?"

"Why not, sire? I can order the royal guards to notify the girl's parents and make the necessary arrangements for the celebration. This girl could be in your bed in just a few hours, ready to satisfy your pleasures."

Beanor appeared to be conflicted: he couldn't recall another wedding being officiated so quickly. He observed the rotundity in front of him. *I can't, I can't wait any longer.*

Observing the king's distant gaze, Tuirl smiled to himself. *But I still need to find out who accused me.*

"Guards!" the king shouted. "Take her to the wives. Have them get her ready for our wedding. And go call her relatives. I want everything ready in less than three hours."

On her way out, the young woman shot Tuirl a look full of hatred.

23

In his laboratory, the wizard Aldin looked about furtively, preparing to pronounce the words of the spell.

A wooden board slid away, displaying the contents of a small closet full of a wide range of objects and scrolls. Aldin pulled out a scroll. He blew the dust off of it, unrolled it, and placed it upon the counter, then double-checked all of the elements he had previously laid out across the table. *It's all here. It took decades of work, but now I have everything I need.* He picked up one thing at a time and used each object to write words in a sacred language through the air. At the same time, he began singing a melody that used those same words, never taking his eyes off of the scroll spread out on the table.

After several long minutes, he felt his body grow lighter. The tone of his voice and the speed at which his hand moved grew in intensity. His hands and arms started to lose their density, becoming transparent. Aldin continued, absorbed in the ritual. Table, floor, ceiling, and wall started to waver until everything vanished completely. Suspended in the void, his skin moist with sweat, he sang the melody with all of the breath remaining in his throat. His fingers flew through the air, so fast that his own eyes could no longer follow their movements. When his body and the room around it regained their consistency, his hands and lips suddenly stopped. The wizard looked around him. The room was empty, as he had expected it would be, so he opened the door and cautiously walked out. He rejoiced, observing the corridor in front of him: *It appears as if His Majesty's forefathers also had good taste.*

He hurried towards the window. Looking out through the glass, he saw three ships hovering over the surface of the sea. Then, one by one, like lightning, they went away.

Perfect timing. They've just left. There's no time to waste.

He padded his way further down the corridor until he heard voices coming from behind a door. *All of the adults are dead in this palace. Could this be...?* He saw the door open and frightened eyes emerge through the crack.

"Zalbia, I told you it isn't one of them! Look at him, you'll see what I mean!"

Aldin immediately knew who that child was. The eyes staring at him and the contours of his face were identical to those of the face in the giant fresco that loomed over the throne room.

"Hurry, children, hurry! They've gone away. Get out of the palace and go find the other survivors!" Aldin encouraged them.

Not needing to be told twice, the children scurried off.

"See? He wasn't one of them!" Moltil commented, elbowing Zalbia.

"B-but if he isn't one of th-them, then who is he?" Brunus asked, trying to keep up with the other two.

The three turned and disappeared around the corner.

Aldin swiftly crossed through rooms, down staircases and corridors. As soon as he stepped outside, he observed the sun's position in the sky. *There's still time.*

He went up the staircase that led to the high walls sheering the sea. There, he turned towards the East: the coast was lost in the distance. The sky was clear and cloudless. The water sparkled. Enchanted, he observed that landscape – the landscape he knew so well, yet that now appeared so entirely different. Many of the villages and roads built over the centuries did not yet exist.

He took an instrument out of his tunic and placed it on the palace wall, calculating a series of coordinates based on the time and place where he stood. He looked around. The palace, as expected, was deserted. Most of the adults had just been exterminated, and the few survivors, mostly women and children, had sought refuge outside of its walls.

Aldin took a few things out of his pocket and started to hum a second melody, writing in the air. The consistency of his body began to fade. Although these elements were rather rare and difficult to find, the ritual for traveling through space was simpler than the ritual for traveling through time.

His limbs, the palace walls, the sea, the sky, the landscape became increasingly transparent and then disappeared.

He found himself in a village, where the smell of scorched wood and smoke made it hard for him to breathe. He was standing in a narrow alley. All of the surrounding houses had been burnt down. A few flames still lapped inside some of the dilapidated buildings. Their roofs had caved in, just like the walls.

Aldin covered his mouth with a handkerchief and tried to make his way through the rubble. Behind the crumbling wall of a house, he noticed several charred bodies. He wondered if it was the fire that had killed them, or if the soldiers had gotten to them first. *They only rebelled because they couldn't pay all those taxes, which were making it hard for them to even survive. And they were punished unjustly.* He wasn't entirely comfortable with the idea of erasing the future of their descendents.

He turned and, now beyond the butchery, continued onwards. The sea and port laid before his eyes. The three ships were already lined up near the shore. The last few stragglers were boarding a fourth ship. A dozen people were still on the pier, busy loading the few things they had been allowed to take with them. Their faces were dazed, bewildered. The women cried. The children sought refuge, hiding underneath their mother's skirts. Their faces were still covered in soot.

This broke Aldin's heart. Beanor was crazy, no doubt about it: but for all of his perverted, homicidal tendencies, he could never have reached the level of brutality of his ancestor. Two thousand years later, the memory of the punishment inflicted upon their people would still be strong.

But I have to do it! He was terrorized by the idea that a priest might survive on the island and undo everything he had worked so hard to arrange. *This will be the coup de grace. Then, finally, I'll be free!*

Standing on the ship and the pier, many continued looking towards the village, as if they could hardly believe what was happening. Aldin hid around the corner of a house, fearing he might be seen.

They keep looking over their former lives, their houses, their happy moments, the nights spent cuddling up with their husband or wife, the evenings at the inn, their holidays...and I killed their future. My showers of stone shards exterminated their descendents. So now I'm here to make sure no one will be able to bring them back to life.

But I can still stop, if I want.

He waited patiently. The last to board was a woman. A man held out his hand to help her. She passed him the bundle of a few things she had managed to save from the massacre and fire. Then the sailors raised the ropes.

The other three ships, in the meantime, had already taken to the waves. The fourth moved away from the pier. Except for the sailors,

71

everyone looked at the village, right in his direction.

I'm not the one responsible for this. It was Beanor's forefather, almost two thousand years before I was born. And if he hadn't exterminated them, the people from the Southern lands wouldn't have intervened, helping the survivors find refuge on the island of Turios, killing the king and the court of Ardis, and finally creating that barrier which, for two thousand years, prevented the people of Isk from sailing South.

I'm just trying to fix everything.

Aldin left his hiding place. Even if someone had seen him from the ship, they certainly couldn't turn back now.

I'm sorry, but I have to do it. Looking towards the sea, he felt as if all of their eyes were staring at him. He felt he could hear their invocations, screaming from the sea, begging him to let them live. Or maybe what he heard were the invocations of the descendents of those men and women who were sailing away, hoping to rebuild their future, which had just been so brutally destroyed.

I could at least let them have the next two thousand years of history. But no, if I do, they could still go back in time, change events and make a new branch of time that, if nourished, would reinvigorate and grow over the one generated by my actions. I'm sorry, but I can't let them stay alive. He drew a circle in the soil in front of him. Aldin removed several herbs, minerals, and a precision instrument from a leather sack. He calculated the measurements around the circle and traced the signs in the proper position. Then he meticulously laid down the herbs and minerals. Holding a scroll, he placed the sack outside of the circle. Finally, very carefully, he placed the scroll in the center of what he had just drawn on the ground.

He started to move his lips. The song, at first a murmur, rose in volume and intensity. He held the scroll down in front of his eyes and, with his other hand, traced the signs in the air.

The wind stopped. The dust remained frozen in the air. The smoke of the burnt structures stopped rising.

Although he was focused on those signs, gestures and songs, his mind was not at peace. *I can still stop. I can leave them their two thousand years of history. That's all they have left. They'll live, love one another, enjoy life, until one day, during a wedding, a shower of stone blades will leave nothing but cadavers all over the ground.*

No, no, no...they could come back here. They might overwrite everything.

He – that horrendous creature who's unworthy of the honor of begging on the street – he went and beat me up in front of everyone; he got down from his throne and struck me repeatedly, under the blank stares of the entire court; me, a wizard, subjected to public humiliation.

But I'm sorry, I have to do it. It's the only way.

Gestures and melodies melted into a single flow which filled the space around him. At the end of the ritual, he pronounced the fateful three words in the sacred language.

On the fourth ship, already far away across the ocean, several wooden beams started creaking. Tiny drops of saltwater seeped through microscopic cracks.

Aldin visualized what would happen over the next six hours: the seepage would weaken the structure of the hulls and the sailors would try, in vain, to repair one leak, while another ten would open within the next moment; the decks of the ship would sink lower and lower to the surface of the water, and the captain would frantically search the nautical maps to see if there was enough time to land on a nearby island or turn back to the port they had just left.

No, they won't have time. I've calculated everything perfectly. You'll be too far from everyone and everything. Nobody will come help you. Nobody in the South will even notice what happened. They'll think you're still heading towards the island of Isk, towards your salvation and your radiant future.

Full of desperation, men, women, and children crowded the deck. As the ship sunk into the sea, a few would try grasping onto scraps of wood, securing a few more minutes of life, as their brothers, sisters, mothers, and fathers would already be in the water, shaking from the cold, listening to their heartbeats slowly fade. The chattering of their teeth would stop and their frozen lips would remain open, unable to let out a last moan of pain, scream for help, or words of useless encouragement for a loved one who, just a little further away, had already died, frozen.

Goodbye, people of Kaj.

24

Bashinoir had fully recovered. Right after breakfast, Lil and Miril went off to start the preparations for the daily ritual. Bashinoir looked forward to when he could return to the forest, walk the paths of the island, stroll along the seashore. He missed the smells and sight of that immense body of water almost as much as the comfort of Lil's warm body underneath the sheets.

I'll be alone. Where I used to spend time with my friends and the other workers, now I'll visit all alone.

He headed towards the front door of the Temple and, after opening it, took a deep breath of the brisk air that whipped against his face. It was a beautiful, bright day. Rays of sunshine filtered through the trees of the forest, bouncing off the dazzling stretch of snow that covered the large square in front of the Temple.

There wasn't a single trace of the cadavers or stone shards.

Bashinoir went down the front staircase, stopping once again to gulp down the fresh air. He instinctively turned Northwest, towards the village, but decided instead to head East. The trails were covered with powdery snow. Once he entered the forest, every tree trunk seemed to remind him of a memory from his past.

When he was younger, he loved playing in the forest. Nothing was more fun than hiding in spots that only he knew about. They were his *dens,* and he felt safe and protected inside of them.

A few years later, still quite young, he had learned to hunt and soon became an infallible predator.

And, among those branches and leaves, he had kissed Lil for the first time. Lil, the woman who became his wife.

She had always been beautiful, even as a little girl. He had spent years courting her, until one day, as they walked along, she looked at him quite candidly and asked: "So, Bashinoir. When are you going to kiss me?" He didn't waste any time, he pulled her close and kissed her, wanting nothing more than to stay with her forever.

And his father? *He taught me so many things in this place.* That man seemed to know every plant, tree, and animal, their most carefully guarded secrets, their curative properties.

"We don't know our future, so we should always be ready for anything," his father used to say. But on that island, far away from everything, what could ever happen to them? Since his people had reached that island, they had prospered in peace. Only children were scared by the legends of the past.

Now, from far away, Bashinoir began to hear the call, the music of the sea. In his mind's eye, he saw the waves crashing against the shore, bathing it, then drawing back again. He felt that once he reached the beach, he would regain the peace he had lost. He walked more quickly, anxious. The fragrance of the sea grew more intense in the air.

The trees thinned and finally the giant mirror of water shone before him. He lowered his eyelids: so much beauty was painful. He took a deep breath and a new energy flowed through him. The strength of that element penetrated every single fiber of his being. It opened him back up. The sun's reflection drew a golden path that led straight to him. He moved forward. The snow covered the beach until just a few steps away from the water. A few rocks jutted out of the water, just a few yards offshore.

The image of Lil, his wife, sitting on that rock and enjoying the heat of a bright, sunny day during the warm season suddenly flooded through his mind. He felt a surge of rage. Why, after everything they had been through, wasn't she here with him? *The rituals, the Temple, the protections. Our survival. Yes, it's right for her to move forward with her new life. Actually, it's necessary.*

He forced himself to think of something else. He couldn't bear the pain anymore. He walked along the shore. After a few hundred feet, the beach was interrupted by a cliff that rose high into the sky. Bashinoir climbed up, observing the forest, the sea, the coast. He made his way through the snow, trying to clear his mind. He thought he could reconnect with himself, alone, in his element. But he had come here so many times before with Lil. He wondered if there was a single spot on the island where the two had never visited together. *But the pain is coming from inside of me, not from out here.* He continued climbing. One particularly large rock stretched out over the sea, now dozens of yards below. It was a splendid panoramic spot, one of his favorites, so he stopped and admired the sea once again. He studied the coast towards the North.

A strange shadow hovered just underneath the surface of the water. He narrowed his eyes. *Is that some sort of big fish?* But large fish didn't swim in that area. The shadow headed towards the coast,

75

below the very spot where he was standing. It was moving in a straight line. *A fish doesn't move that way.*

Bashinoir knelt down on the snow, placing his hands on the rocky ground before him to get a better look. The shadow had an irregular shape to it – shifting, ambiguous. It was somewhat round, but it continually changed. *No, that's not a fish. It's...something else.*

Once it was directly below him, he leaned down even further. The shape stopped moving.

Intrigued, Bashinoir stared at it. He almost felt as if the shadow were returning his gaze, making him feel strangely intimidated. *No, what am I thinking? It's got to be some sort of marine animal. I'm just too high up to be able to see it clearly.*

He noticed that he felt lighter, calmer, and more relaxed than he had in ages. His thoughts flowed freely, as if an old woman were narrating an ancient story: the shower of the deathly sharp rock shards, the disappearance of the cadavers, the priestess, the Temple, Lil's last embrace. But the anguish and the desperation that had overwhelmed him until just a few moments ago had disappeared. The agonizing twinge from the wound on his calf had vanished. Once again, he studied the shadow below him. The waves made it bob up and down. It suddenly moved off, not further down the coast, but out to the open sea.

Desolation ripped through his soul like a flooding river. The stress of recent events and his sad condition came crashing down upon him, until he found it hard to breathe and his eyes watered. He brought a hand to his calf, where the wound had resumed pulsating with pain.

25

"Master, through my projection I found a man walking along the shore!"

Intrigued, Obolil lifted his gaze towards the apprentice who, rising from the cot, was speaking very animatedly, his eyes shining with excitement.

Already? "Are you sure? Or was it just an illusion, one of the few things foolish old Aldin seems to have left as his legacy?"

Ilis hesitated. *What if he was right? In all fairness, he hadn't mastered the astral voyage, much less long-distance projections. But he had felt that sensation so clearly...*

In front of Ilis' uncertain eyes, Obolil lost his patience. "Come on, boy. Tell me what happened."

Ilis took a deep breath, trying to find the courage to recall what had just happened: "I was in the astral dimension, and I stopped on this side of the barrier, as you ordered me to. I sent a projection towards the coast of the island. This time, I was able to distinctly sense the beaches, the rocks, and the trees. I started to circumnavigate the coast, until I felt that I could perceive a human frequency not too far away. I tried to get closer, but my projection is still very weak and I was unable to move it out from under the water. The man was at a very high point of the coast, but it seemed as if he were kneeling down to look in my direction."

Hmm...if this is true, it would indeed be extraordinary. I never would have imagined that this boy could progress so quickly. Ah, if only he hadn't wasted his best years caught up in foolish games with that incompetent Aldin!

Ilis examined the wizard's expression, hoping he had finally made a positive impression. "And his thoughts? Were you able to perceive them?" Obolil asked brusquely.

"N-no, master. But as I mentioned, the man was very high up. I could only detect a few emotions." He wanted to continue, but the wizard's sneering expression snuffed out any enthusiasm he had felt over the success of his mission.

"And so? What kind of emotions did that man feel?"

Ilis, increasingly insecure, tried to respond: "Well, see...I got the impression that he felt very alone. And unhappy...well, really unhappy. I felt that he was having a horrible day, even though the place where he was standing gave him a certain level of comfort."

Good, good.

"Good, good. So try to project yourself to that point more often. He might come back, and you'd better be there waiting for him. When he noticed your projection, how did he react?"

"Well, I got the feeling he was curious. I did what you taught me to do and I emanated a flow of positive energy. It was very tiring, but I think he felt the effect."

If only I could have been there! Obolil regretted no longer having the strength needed for such long astral voyages.

"If you get another chance to meet him, you need to attract him down to a lower point along the coast. Move slowly, so he'll come and follow you. Try to bring him to a place where you can read his thoughts. Once you manage to do that, don't go overboard. Use a very light touch, he shouldn't pick up on what you're doing. Read everything you can. No more than a few minutes. Send out a sensation of warmth towards him, and then come immediately back and report to me. We need to make him come back as much as possible, hopefully every day. Once we thoroughly understand his thoughts and what his soul longs for, we'll figure out how to manipulate him."

Maybe he really is impressed but doesn't want me to know that, the apprentice consoled himself.

26

Sitting at the table in the large kitchen, Lil gulped down her husband's words. Bashinoir had told them about everything he had done that day. He had explored the island, looking for evidence of any changes, but didn't notice anything in particular. He had gone to the village. The houses were cold and abandoned. Everything had stayed the way it was on the day the stone shards rained down. He had taken care of the animals which, although starving, had all survived in their stables. And he had started to build a new structure close to the Temple. From the way he was talking, it seemed as if Bashinoir were anxious to finish the job. *Maybe he just doesn't want to go back to the village again.*

As Lil listened to him talk about his time outside of the Temple, she felt a lump in her throat. She looked at Miril, thankful that the priestess didn't seem to notice her emotions.

Bashinoir didn't say anything about their old house and she didn't have the courage to ask about it.

"Good," Miril said with a slight smile. "It's very comforting to know that the animals are in good health."

Those words caught Bashinoir and Lil by surprise. When had a priestess ever cared about the health of a bunch of animals?

Lil felt slightly embarrassed. She wished she could find a way to lighten up the evening. After all, they were alive, so they had the duty to try to be at least a little bit cheerful. However, Bashinoir and Miril, despite his respectful attitude and her smiles, seemed to belong to a far away world. "Want to listen to a song?" Lil asked them.

Bashinoir and the priestess turned towards her; he was surprised, and she was serene.

"Of course, why not?" Miril responded.

Lil stood up, moved towards the hearth, made a quick curtsy and started to sing a melody she had learned from her mother.

It was a legend about her people, narrating how their ancestors, once they had landed on Turios after escaping from Isk by sea, had started building houses and the Temple. As they built new houses to keep them warm, the first nucleus of the Temple—nothing more than a circle of stones laid out in a meadow—had protected them

79

enough that they could live in peace.

It was a beautiful melody, imbued with hopeful emotions and dreams for the future.

As she sang, Lil observed Bashinoir, who appeared to be moved. The music touched him. Once she finished, Lil made another curtsy.

"They were an entire tribe. They were escaping from their land and they chose to settle down here. But there are only *three* of us," Bashinoir thought aloud.

He was the first to be surprised by his own words. He never would have imagined he could express himself so freely in the presence of the priestess.

"Bashinoir, what do you think we can do?" she asked.

He understood that he couldn't back down from expressing his point of view. "Perhaps, priestess, we should take to the sea. I spent a long time looking at it today. I saw its splendor and I felt the promises that it holds. Perhaps we would die, in fact we probably would, but what do we have to look forward to here?"

He feels alone. Miril and I spend all day working on the tiring ritual protections, we don't even have time to think about these kinds of things, Lil thought.

"It is a possibility," Miril replied. "However, we don't have any nautical maps, not to mention a ship. Our ancestors got rid of everything because they wanted to stay on this island. Sometimes I wonder if there is a higher meaning to the isolation within which they voluntarily constrained us, not to mention the strength of the protection rituals for the Temple. In any case, they didn't want to return to the seas."

She knows a whole lot more than what she's willing to tell us. Since Lil had begun studying with Miril, she had begun to notice how much the priestess knew about the world, and how her understanding of it differed from their vision.

The two women and the man were exhausted from the day's hard work. Bashinoir, after hearing her answer, considered the matter settled and politely took his leave. After Miril and Bashinoir had gone off, Lil took care of a few chores before retiring to her own room.

This was her least favorite time of the evening. Spending the day in the company of Miril was comforting – often tiring, and sometimes she felt that she wouldn't be able to keep going, but those tasks helped keep her mind busy. Now, however, alone in her room with her own thoughts, she was once again wrapped in sadness and melancholy.

A gentle knock on the door made her flinch.

"I saw the light shining under the door and assumed you were still awake. Are you having trouble sleeping, Lil?" Miril asked. She was wearing her nightgown, her hair undone.

Despite all the time they spent together, Lil still wasn't too comfortable talking about personal things. "It's no big deal. I'm just having a hard time getting used to my new home."

"As well as this sense of solitude, I imagine?" the woman asked, smiling.

"Actually, yes," Lil admitted. "I've slept beside him for so many years. And before then, I slept with my sisters."

"I see." Miril continued smiling at her tenderly. "Would you prefer to have some company?"

Lil's eyes grew wide. *Why is she asking me that? She was the one who made it clear that, once I started out as a novice, I would no longer be able to lie beside Bashinoir. Has something changed?* A spark of hope ignited deep within her soul. "Yes, I would," she revealed, not without a hint of embarrassment.

"Do you want me to come sleep with you?"

Lil was dumbfounded: that wasn't the suggestion she was expecting. She hoped the priestess wouldn't feel offended by the astonishment that was undoubtedly written all over her face. "That w-would be nice; but I didn't think that was okay..." Her words seemed strange. *I'm definitely offending her now.*

"We already slept together. Remember the first nights in front of the fireplace?" Miril continued calmly, noticing Lil's agitation.

"Yes, but now..." Lil realized it would be stupid to question Miril's words. "That'd be very nice," she hurried to correct herself. She wasn't Bashinoir, but it still would be so much better than solitude. She couldn't hold back a deep sigh.

"Alright. Can you make a little room for me?"

Miril seemed rather happy. Lil moved over to one side of the bed and the other woman laid down next to her.

Lil felt tense, but she didn't toss or turn. Miril smelled so good. Her hair had the scent of floral essences.

Maybe she really is happy. This is probably something new and pleasant for her, Lil reflected.

The fatigue from the day got the better of her and Lil let herself fall into a deep, peaceful sleep.

She woke up during the night, cold. In the darkness, she realized the fire had gone out. She wondered, half-asleep, if she should start another fire, but a warm arm comforted her and she fell asleep once again, content.

27

King Beanor nervously drummed his fingers against the arm of his throne. The large ceremonial hall was sumptuously decorated. The nobles of the city had come running as soon as the royal guards notified them of the event. Almost all of the king's wives were present. A few were still busy giving orders to the servants, who were trying to prepare the family members of the girl the king was about to marry.

Beanor motioned for the advisor Tuirl, seated in the first row, to come closer: "How much longer is this going to take? I've already been waiting for a half hour!"

Tuirl shrugged his shoulders: "Your Highness, we have managed to arrange a wedding in just a few hours during the middle of the evening. All of the nobles rushed over here. The tailors, however, are still working on the clothes for Milia's family members, who unfortunately didn't have anything appropriate to wear."

"Milia? Who's that?"

"Your Highness! It's the name of your future wife!"

"Oh." said Beanor, impatient. *I want to fuck her! I want that nice little ass in my hands! I want to see her bend down in front of me! And then make her pay for forcing me to wait for so long.*

A royal guard, breathless, came forward and respectfully asked to speak with the king and his advisor.

"Yes, yes, go on!" Beanor, annoyed, granted him permission.

"Your Majesty, we can't find the girl's father! The wife told us he was coming back from a business trip. We went to meet him on the road he usually takes. We should have crossed paths with him at an inn no more than an hour from here by horse, thinking we could then bring him back for the wedding, but we didn't find him. The owner told us that, due to the bad weather, her father probably hadn't been able to get over the Sclir hill. Unfortunately, the first town on the other side of that hill is over six hours away by horse." The guard spoke quickly, without pausing. The king's impatience was legendary and everyone knew that if he wasn't pleased with an explanation, he was capable of highly unusual reactions.

Tuirl remained silent. The king glared at the guard.

"And so? Now what do we do?"

"Your Majesty, tradition requires the bride's father to be present," the advisor reminded him.

Damn weather! Beanor thought of the girl's curves. He was so close! He had ordered an especially brief ceremony. As soon as the solemn vows were pronounced, when the nobles and their wives would begin to guzzle down all the food and drink he had paid for, he would take her to one of the tunnels behind the main hall. He couldn't think of anything he liked more than taking a young woman, slamming her against the hard ground or a wall and filling her with all of his virility, as her virginal blood ran down her thighs, a muffled scream trying to make its way through the fingers that covered her mouth, her head squirming underneath the hand that pulled her hair back.

Beanor couldn't think of anything else: he was already so close, he couldn't give up now. The image of the young woman's rump continued to torment him. "We must have the wedding without the father, then. Advisor, have the girl's family brought forward, wearing whatever they're wearing. We'll begin the ceremony."

"Your Majesty, tradition does not allow for you to take a young woman as your wife in the absence of her father, unless..."

Why does this blockhead dare to contradict me?

"...the girl is an orphan. But we know that Milia's father is alive."

For the love of the gods! Why does everything always work against me? I'm the king! Can't people just do what I tell them to do?

"Advisor," Beanor retorted, with a threatening gaze. "This stupid wedding was all your idea. So you need to find a solution, unless you want me to kick your ass in front of the entire court!"

Tuirl looked around, embarrassed. He had no idea how to resolve the problem and Beanor's mood was visibly growing worse. Luckily, the hall packed with illustrious guests would probably prevent him from going too far.

If I have to do everything myself anyway, what do I need this idiot for?

Suddenly Beanor beamed, overjoyed after discovering what he considered to be a brilliant solution: "We'll declare the father dead! Then we can proceed with the ceremony!" he exclaimed, satisfied, sure that his stroke of genius had resolved the issue.

Tuirl softly objected: "But your Majesty, the girl's father is not dead."

"Tuirl, you yokel, where's your imagination? I know he's alive, but we'll just say we went out looking for him before the wedding and someone at the inn told us he died in an accident on his way here!"

"If that is what you wish, your Highness, that's what we'll do. But allow me to point out that her father may come back tomorrow, or the day after. And that would certainly create a scandal."

These nobles, they're always watching, always ready to judge me! They fear me, but as soon as I'm out of earshot, they all talk behind my back. He hadn't thought that the father might actually come back.

He dismissed the guard, who had remained standing, frozen, a few steps away, and motioned for Tuirl to come closer. "Then do what needs to be done to make sure he doesn't come back."

Tuirl's eyes grew wide: "Your Majesty, what are you saying? We can't have the father of your future wife killed!"

Beanor's hands itched. He wanted to lash out against someone or something, but the hall was crawling with guests and it didn't seem like the right moment. He tried to concentrate. *Hmm, let's get back to the main issue: I have to fuck that girl. Now or very soon.*

The image of those buttocks continued to torment him. So compact, so well-proportioned, pure, never before touched. He tried to distract himself, thinking instead about her legs, her delicate ankles, her tiny little feet, her sensual face, her lips created expressly to wrap around his member.

And that girl, whose name he didn't quite remember, seemed to emanate a slightly impudent attitude. She really was the type of damsel he adored domesticating. He'd bring ones like her into bed, force them to endure incredible obscenities and, once they dared to rebel, he knew exactly what to do to break them. He felt he needed to get started on this right away, he couldn't wait any longer.

He looked at the group of his well-fed wives. Could he console himself with one of them instead? Or even three or four? No. He knew his obsession was stronger than he was. And he knew that, until he had reached his goal, he would not find any peace.

"What if instead of killing him, we just send him into exile?"

Tuirl seemed even more perplexed than before. "Sire, if we declare Milia's father dead now, the news would transform the wedding into a funeral. The laments, cries, and sobs of the family

85

members would ruin the ceremony. And the young woman really wouldn't be in the best of moods. You'd risk losing sight of your goal completely. A girl distraught by the death of her father is not exactly the type of conquest one aspires towards."

Beanor tried to imagine the scene: the wife dressed in black, sprawled out on the floor, sobbing uncontrollably, as he moved closer to her with his penis erect. He would kneel down in front of her, yank her head up by her hair and force her tear-strewn face to look at him. She would gaze at him, begging. He would whisper that she would feel better soon and then push the tip of his member between her lips. She would still be sobbing desperately but would start to do her duty, until he exploded in ecstasy between her lips and all over her face: the semen would mix with her tears.

Actually the scenario didn't displease him.

28

Prince Beanor returned to his bedroom, holding his birthday gift.

"Oh, sorry, prince. I didn't realize you'd be coming back so soon. I'll clear out of here immediately," said Braila, one of his servants.

"No, no, carry on. I...I couldn't wait to get back and read the book Father gave me. My birthday celebration will resume within a few hours."

"Indeed. It must be a lovely book," the woman observed, gazing at the inlaid leather cover.

"It is, see? It's got all of the kings from the last two thousand years."

"Oh...how wonderful! And one day the master scribe will also add you. And then I'm sure you'll be far too busy to suffer conversations with your servants."

"But no," Beanor responded, flattered. "What are you saying? I'll be a good king, close to all of my subjects, just like my grandpa Bolis IV."

Braila smiled, gave him a wink and continued dusting the bookshelves, turning her back to him.

The prince jumped on his bed, the precious book in his hand.

He read the first pages and started to daydream. *One day I'll be king and the scribes will faithfully write down everything I do. Everyone will be able to read about the accomplishments of the great and invincible Beanor! I'll take down the barrier and conquer the islands and the Southern lands!*

Braila worked on the other side of the room, her back still to him. Her emerald green skirt hung down to her ankles. Her black hair was swept back in a braid. The prince gazed at her, watching her movements.

She turned around: "Do you need something?"

How did she know I was watching her? Beanor wondered. "N-no. I was just thinking."

"Ah." She resumed her work and the prince immersed himself once again in the book.

"And is there a young lady who has already conquered the prince's heart?" Braila asked nonchalantly, a moment later.

"No. I mean...I don't think about those kinds of things," the young man replied, thoroughly embarrassed. *Maybe I should ask her to leave me alone.* But her presence in the room comforted him.

He went back to his book. From time to time, he watched Braila out of the corner of his eye. After a while, she came towards his bed to dust the nightstand.

The young Beanor pretended to be absorbed in his book. He found her proximity unsettling.

"And what is his Majesty reading now?"

"Well, this part is about King Atril XIII, who led an expedition North to try and find a path out of isolation."

"Ah! That would be the gentleman with the long mustache but no beard whose picture hangs in the Hall of Kings?"

"Yes. And see, there's another portrait of him in my book."

Braila bent over to look. Involuntarily, the boy's eye was drawn to her generous bust. He immediately looked away.

"Oh, he must have been a terrific king, just like all the others in your family."

"Yes, he's one of my favorites, even though that courageous expedition cost him his life."

"Really? What happened?"

"Unfortunately he never came back, just like the three expeditions sent by his son to search for him."

"Oh, those poor men! I'm sure that once you're king, you'll continue your father's work and finally be the one to bring down that barrier."

Beanor gleamed, enjoying the woman's faith in him. She had known him forever and always cheered him on with her encouraging words.

"At any rate, you're already a very promising young man," Braila added, standing at the side of the bed.

"You think so?"

"Of course. Who wouldn't?" The women knew about the young boy's insecurities.

"Well, I'm never the best in my lessons. And my father the king looks at me without saying a word. Sometimes his eyes are so mean they scare me." He didn't open up to very many people: this servant was one of those few.

"Oh, Prince Beanor. The king is proud of his son, he just doesn't want to say it aloud. That's how he is. There are a lot of things on his mind. He has a gruff personality, but there's no doubt he loves you."

Beanor badly wanted his father to say something kind to him, but he couldn't remember ever hearing a nice word from him.

A tear fell down his cheek and onto the book, staining the portrait of King Atril.

"What's this, now? Don't get upset. There, there, now. I remember when I used to hold you when you were little. And now look at what a handsome young man you've become," Braila consoled, coming closer to give him a hug.

Beanor's face pressed against that generous bosom and he stopped crying, cheered by the reassuring contact.

When the woman let go, the prince continued staring at her chest.

She let him do as he pleased, commenting, after a few moments: "Hmm. I get the feeling women *are* starting to capture your interest."

Beanor immediately realized he was staring. "Oh, well, I...I'm sorry, I didn't mean to do that."

"You didn't do anything wrong. Have you ever seen one of these?" she asked him, nodding towards her breasts.

"N-no, I mean...no. I mean...not that I remember."

"Oh, well, it's really no big deal. But if you want, given that it's your birthday..."

The boy's eyes grew wide. That would be great, yes of course! But he didn't dare respond.

"Well? I suppose you're still not interested. One day you will be, though," Braila concluded, taking a step back.

Beanor lifted his hand towards her: "Wait! Please! Yes, I want to see...what they're like."

Braila smiled, pleased, and left, to the prince's great disappointment, but only to go and latch the door shut. "Perhaps it's better that nobody disturbs you during your exam."

The prince swallowed, wondering what she expected him to do at that point. He remained frozen.

Braila came closer and sat on the edge of the bed. Very slowly, she started to untie the laces of the white shirt she wore underneath her emerald dress. When they were all opened, looking the boy right in the eyes, she asked him: "So. Are you curious?"

"Y-yes, please, open it."

The woman pulled her shirt down and to the side. One of her splendid breasts popped out.

Beanor felt a vortex of emotions wash over him. Short on breath, he managed only to say: "They're very nice. I mean...they're...nice."

Braila smiled. "You think so? I'm delighted."

The young man lifted his right hand but immediately withdrew it. Then, feeling brave, he dared to ask her: "Can I touch?"

"Well you really shouldn't. But given that it's your birthday..."

"Thanks," Beanor said, lifting his trembling hand and gently placing it on Braila's breast.

"Seems like you already know how to touch a woman. It also appears as if you're not displeased," she commented, referring to the immense erection that pressed against the flap of his pants.

"Oh...sure," Beanor immediately withdrew his hand. "It's just...sorry...I mean, I didn't want -"

"No, what's the matter? There's nothing wrong with that. Do you ever touch it?" Braila asked.

"Yes. I mean no." The young man was completely confused.

"For more than a few seconds?" she asked, trying to understand.

"No, of course not."

Perhaps he hasn't before, she thought. "Perhaps there's something I can teach you. Carry on with your caresses."

He took a hand and placed it on her soft breast. Then she opened his pants and slowly started to stroke the young man's member while looking into his eyes.

He was immediately transported into ecstasy. He had entered a new world, a valley full of smells and marvels that he had never experienced before. The woman's black pupils, now as big as the sky, hovered above him.

He felt all of his energy move from his limbs, his stomach, and every other part of his body towards his pelvis, like a gigantic river which, suddenly, flooded that magical place. He was unable to resist the woman's pressing movement. He saw a white liquid shoot out of his member, spurting so high as to hit her in the face.

He felt drained, as if something had sucked all the energy out of his body and mind. Then he started laughing. He laughed as he had never laughed in his life before. This new world was a dimension he never, ever wanted to leave. There was no comparison to it. There was nothing better than this. He wanted to embrace her, but he held himself back, not knowing how a prince should act under these circumstances. She cleaned her face off with her fingers. Then she took a handkerchief from a pocket in her skirt and dried off her hands.

"Did you like that?"

"Oh, Braila, that was stupendous. It's the best thing that ever happened to me. I love you. I feel...I feel that you're the woman of my life."

Braila internally smiled at the young man's sweet innocence. "Want to do it again some other time?" she asked, moving closer to his face.

"I'd like that very much. You're the most marvelous creature I've ever seen in my life."

"So," she said, suddenly strict, frightening him, "you must never, for any reason, under any circumstances, tell anybody what just happened. Do you understand?"

"Y-yes, of course. As you wish," he said, intimidated.

"Now, if you keep this secret, if you don't tell anyone about what just happened, then I'll let you enjoy many, many more pleasures even nicer than this," she continued, once again sweet and gentle.

"As you wish," he replied, unable to think of anything that would make him happier.

29

"He came back, and we...communicated."

Ilis didn't know if he should feel happy over the incredible connection he had just experienced, or terrified of the corporal punishment his master would certainly inflict upon him for disobeying orders.

"I know, I know. Sorry," he hastened to say, "I made a mistake. But it was going so well and I thought it would be a shame not to take advantage of the moment."

Intent upon preparing his potions, Obolil was bent over the table and surrounded by all sorts of ingredients and minerals. He finally looked at the apprentice without saying a word. Ilis expected him to explode with rage but instead, the wizard seemed calm, even curious.

"You spoke with the man on the island? And what did you talk about?" he muttered.

"Well, see. I was waiting patiently, in the usual spot," Ilis started to explain, running a hand through his brown hair. "I started to sense his presence when he was still rather far away from the coast, so I sent him a wave of emotion, as you taught me to. I think this attracted him towards me, since he came almost immediately afterwards."

Obolil let out a gasp of dismay. Though he wanted to continue, Ilis stopped, afraid of the scolding he was about to receive.

"I told you to send him comforting emotions *after* entering into contact with him, not before." Obolil would have gladly gotten up to slap the young man around a little but, feeling tired, decided to yield to curiosity instead. "Alright. Well, go on."

"So," Ilis continued, his enthusiasm winning over his fear of the master's cruelty, "as I said, the man came towards me. But he was still too high up, so I kept sending waves of emotion. I lured him down to a lower spot on the rocks." Ilis took a breath, excited by the next part. "It was fantastic. Once I was near him, I could read him like a book."

"Could you *distinctly* perceive his thoughts?" Obolil asked, unconvinced.

"His thoughts? Not just those, master: I could go all the way back through his memory!"

How is that possible? I haven't taught him that yet, and there's no way he could have picked that up on his own.

"Interesting. But are you sure this isn't just one of your delusions?"

"Do you think it could be? Let me tell you what I found out, then."

Ilis realized he had succeeded in persuading his master: his self-esteem shot through the roof. More excited than ever, he told Obolil about Bashinoir's memories, dwelling upon the shower of stone shards and the time he had spent convalescing in the Temple.

Those aren't the kinds of ideas a boy invents, Obolil realized as he wrung his wrinkled hands.

Once Ilis finished telling his story, he remained silent, anticipating what the wizard would have to say.

"Three. So there are three of them left."

"Exactly, master. And one of them is a priestess. So that's why the island is still being protected!"

"Yes. But you told me Aldin thought they were all at the wedding."

"Right. When Master Aldin prepared the spell for the stone assault, he thought all of the islanders were at the wedding, as he had seen during a projection. He said they created a magical circle that guaranteed strength and vitality to the future couple. He said even the sick, the newly born, and the elderly came to those kinds of celebrations."

That makes sense. There were so few of them, even before, that they needed to use every last bit of vital energy as best they could. They certainly couldn't let problems arise between couples. These weddings were probably even arranged by the priests according to a plan that helped them avoid interbreeding, as much as it could be avoided.

"But that's not what happened. According to the man's memory, it seems as if he and his wife had been saved by an incredible twist of fate. And the priestess had stayed inside of the Temple," Ilis continued.

So it was her. The only one who could have maintained the protections of the Temple. Did she suspect something? "Maybe the priestess knew something was going to happen. That's why she

93

didn't participate in the celebration."

The apprentice observed his master, surprised. "What makes you say that?"

"Listen, dear apprentice. It's the sort of doubt anyone could have." Ilis was shocked by the unusually kind way the master spoke – he even seemed to be smiling. "Think about that man. He's lost everything. Now he suspects that woman is taking away his wife. On a rational level, he probably understands that it's all necessary. But emotionally, he's suffering. It wouldn't take much more for him to start questioning the priestess. He doesn't have anything to go by, but if you infuse such doubts in his mind, you'd give him the pretext he doesn't yet know to look for."

"You want me to make him think the priestess knew about the stone shards?"

"No, quite the contrary. You don't need to make him think anything. You need to act like you're interested and ask questions so he generates the doubt on his own."

Ilis started to understand his master's plan. He had thought Aldin worked in a rather underhanded manner, but now Obolil seemed even more wicked.

"That idiot Aldin could have worked to make sure they would break up on their own, that they'd disrupt the delicate balance their society has been based on for two thousand years. We should have pitted them all against one another instead of wasting decades searching for magical ingredients that are almost impossible to find."

"Master, what should our goal be? What should happen once the man starts to doubt his priestess?"

"Nothing. Let the doubt take root and prosper, along with his anxiety. From what you've told me, he spends his days almost completely alone. The women are busy with the rituals, logically, given the enormous magical protections they have to sustain. He'll come looking for you more often. Your projection will be the only friendly voice in his life. Just be a shadow and a voice in his mind: that's all you need to drive a man mad, anyway. When he's unstable enough, and when suspicion of the priestess has poisoned his soul, we'll awaken his greed for what used to be his: the wife. And we'll help him win her back."

"But how?"

Obolil looked Ilis up and down. *He helped Aldin prepare the stone assault. He's got to be ready for this as well.*

"Kill the priestess."

30

In one of the large ritual halls of the Temple, Lil arranged candles and sticks of incense. The dim light from the flames mixed with the solitary ray of sunshine that filtered through the single, narrow opening located at the very top of the majestic room. Lil delighted in the spicy odor that emanated from the thin wisps of smoke.

She had almost reached the middle of the room. She stopped to admire her surroundings, unable to conceive how a people as small as her own had been able to construct such impressive architecture.

The walls of the circular room rose dozens of yards high; an elegant array of columns created a concentric circle a few feet away from its perimeter. Every inch of the wall surface was decorated with a dense mosaic that narrated the history of her people, from the time when they fled the Kingdom of Isk until the present day.

Everywhere she looked, the detailed depictions were full of esoteric symbols and letters from ancient languages.

"One day you'll be able to understand all of this," Miril had told her.

Yet Lil's heart ached as she thought about how nobody would be able to continue building upon this great structure. Her people had always dedicated themselves to working on the Temple. One by one, men and women of all ages had devoted their talents to the Temple: some focused on the mosaics, others on the paintings, others on the building construction itself.

And now? It's all over! Lil lamented, unable to keep the sad thoughts at bay. She thought about Miril, who had spent her entire life in this place. Since she had become a priestess, she had directed these sorts of works. How could she support the fact that these rooms, until just recently full of sweat and toil, had taken on such a deep, yet mournful silence? Yet looking at her, it seemed as if nothing had changed. That couldn't be further from the truth, of course: now they were alone, and they couldn't go on struggling forever to stay alive.

She wiped a tear away with the back of her hand and returned to her work, adding candles to the altar of a god who appeared in the form of a child. This room was dedicated to him. Lil knew one of his many names, Nibielaz. "With every level of consciousness, you will learn new concepts. Even the mastery of the names of the gods is part of your training," Miril had explained.

A hand gently brushed her forearm, making her flinch. "Oh! It's you!" she exclaimed.

"Were you expecting somebody else?" the priestess asked, smiling.

"No, actually." *Who else could it be?*

"I brought you something. You can try it on." Miril handed her a green, ceremonial dress.

"Did you make it, priestess?" *Is this the dress that one day she'll let me wear?* Lil didn't dare get her hopes up.

"Yes, I just finished it."

Lil looked at her, surprised: her face was tired, but beaming. She had never seen Miril sewing during the day, so she had probably sacrificed her nighttime sleep in order to work on it. "Why?" she asked, apprehensively.

"Because it's time for your initiation."

That can't be right. "My initiation? But...I don't think I'm ready."

"You are," Miril reassured her, "and from now on, you'll also take part in the rituals."

"Oh." Lil was shocked.

"We can get started."

"Now?" Lil asked, bewildered.

"But of course. This is where it happens, in front of Nibielaz, the god this room is dedicated to. He is the god who symbolizes the mysteries you'll be initiated under."

Lil turned towards the altar, uncertain. "Him?"

"Yes. Don't be fooled by appearances, there's a lot to learn about this Temple. His altar seems very similar to the altars of so many other gods but, in reality, his energy is what flows through this Temple. He's the one you need to merge with. Now, kneel in front of the altar."

Lil's heart began racing. What was going to happen? She wanted to escape and go back to her old life, with Bashinoir, her parents, her friends. *I'm not ready for this.* But she knelt down. Miril stood next to her.

In a sacred language, the priestess pronounced a series of words Lil didn't understand. The longer she listened, however, the more she felt that she could infer their meaning: not with her mind, but with her heart. It was as if the words materialized in the space between them and the altar. She could see them dancing, gracefully, elegantly.

In the language of their people, Miril asked her if she was ready to die, to leave herself behind and be reborn in the cult of the god Nibielaz.

Lil remained quiet, uncertain. *Why didn't Miril prepare me for all of this? Why does this have to happen so suddenly?* Yet on an intuitive level, she felt this was how it was supposed to go. *Life gives us gifts and brings us pain when we least expect it.*

"Yes," she responded simply.

Miril finished the initiation ritual by pronouncing a series of magical formulas. But Lil didn't need to listen any longer. The energy of that magnificent place had begun to flow through her. She closed her eyes.

Yes, let it carry you away. Savor what you feel. Allow the god's energy to flow through you.

She whispered. "You...can communicate through thoughts?"

Yes. And now you can hear me. It's one of the powers that the god gives us. You can try it for yourself.

Lil, her eyes closed, concentrated. *Like this? Can you...hear me? Perfectly.*

The intensity of the energy flowed through every part of her body and soul. Lil felt so full, and yet so light, that she could almost hover in the air. *I've never felt anything like this. It's phenomenal.*

It usually takes years of preparation, but you got to this level in a matter of weeks. You've worked very hard. You've dedicated yourself to this duty wholeheartedly, and this is the result. There's no level of initiation that you won't be able to reach, if you remain this committed.

Lil couldn't keep her doubts to herself. *Priestess, what does all of this mean? There are only three of us left. We're destined to a life of solitude. We've lost everything.*

Lil, I know what torments you, Miril responded, *but if we survived, there's a reason why, and we have the duty to understand it. We need to live this life as best we can. This is the second time we have received the gift of life: the first upon our birth, and the second when we escaped the terrible event during which all of our brothers and sisters perished. Now that you've been initiated, embrace the flow of events. It's what's brought you this great gift.*

Did everyone she loved have to be sacrificed in order for her to be initiated? Lil wondered.

Lil, the reality we experience is in the now. What happened, for better or worse, has led to this moment. It's now up to us to do our best, every moment of our lives. As a new initiate of the god Nibielaz, you've shown that you know how to direct your energy to something higher and more important than simple regret over what you've lost.

A new sense of awareness awoke within her. *You're right, priestess. Please pardon my doubts. I'll devote myself body and soul to this path towards enlightenment.*

I know, Lil. I can see, in your eyes, in your soul, what you truly aspire to.

Miril came closer and gave her a sisterly hug, then took her head in her hands and, lowering it gently, kissed her forehead.

The girl felt the Temple's energy flow even more intensely upon that contact. Her forehead was on fire. She felt happy. For the first time in her life, she felt whole, complete.

31

Bashinoir struggled to place one foot in front of the other. He panted as he walked along the path that wound higher and higher through the trees of the forest. Every once in a while, he looked behind him. He was far away, perhaps too far, but he continued onwards. He wasn't headed in a specific direction.

He thought again about Lil and the priestess Miril. *I wish...I really wish I could take care of you.*

That day, he should have been working on finishing up the new stables so the animals could be moved into the Temple's protection as soon as possible. But, as he had been doing more frequently, he had decided to forget about his duties.

Every day he woke up, convinced he could hang on. He knew how important it was for each one of them to pull their weight, but when it was time to get to work, he suddenly found himself unmotivated and unwilling. He wasn't sure where the anxieties and fears that plagued him came from. Instead of working, he wandered through the forest, losing himself in all sorts of unproductive activities such as sitting on the beach for hours, or wandering through the hills. Sometimes he did the minimum necessary, other times he didn't do anything at all.

During the evenings, the two women seemed very positive and full of energy, despite their fatigue, and would ask him how he had spent his day. Feeling guilty, he tried to remain vague, often lying, wishing they would just drop the subject. They did what they could to share their joy and love with him, and he promised himself he would try harder the next day.

Sometimes, before getting to work, Bashinoir would try to inspire his strength and willpower by picturing Lil and Miril. They were the last hope of his people, all that remained, and they depended upon him for their material survival.

But even then, he couldn't bring himself to do anything. He gave himself another day off and wandered around aimlessly. *Tomorrow...tomorrow I'll do my best. Tomorrow I'll get to work, this time for sure.*

He had climbed so high up that his footsteps crunched through thick masses of snow. It would take a lot of effort to continue

100

onwards.

He invented new goals and new limits. *There, once I get to that point up there, I'll start heading back.* But as soon as he reached that point, he would continue walking all the same, setting his eyes on a new goal to reach further along.

He felt like a teenager, escaping from life to hang around the trees, laughing, joking, lurking around the path, waiting for a girl to pass by. But in his case, he knew that nobody would ever pass by.

Maybe I just can't do this. Maybe everything that's happened has made it impossible for me to work again. I could try working half the day and spend the other half resting, he hypothesized as he continued climbing up. It was a good idea, but he knew, deep down, that he wouldn't follow through with that idea.

He stopped once he left the forest. From then onwards, the path was no longer covered by the trees.

He observed the contours of the island. Mountains, woods, meadows, everything was covered with snow. He looked up. *Did a spell so evil that it exterminated all those I love really come from that sky?*

He tried to quell his anxiety with a piece of dry bread. Suddenly, somewhat shamefully, he became aware of his body: he was putting on weight.

Whenever he combed through the now-empty houses to collect provisions, before bringing them back to the Temple, he would stop in the forest and eat. He was trying to stuff his nervousness deeper down. He wanted to stop, but he kept on until he felt like he could burst, when a sense of nausea came over him. He then felt so full that, at dinner, he could barely swallow down whatever Lil had cooked. Looking along the coast, he saw, in the distance, the point where she was waiting for him: the shadow. He felt the compelling need to go see her. She was one of his few comforts left. He knew she probably wasn't real, but the illusion made him feel good. When he was with her, his anxiety and tension disappeared, even if he was slightly afraid of the ambiguous feelings that came over him in her presence.

There were times when he wanted to escape from her and stay far, far away from everything: from the homes of his dead relatives and friends in the village, from his wife, from the priestess, from the shadow, from the past.

He continued walking. He knew that path by memory; otherwise, with all that snow, it would have been easy to get lost.

The sky was turning dark. It had begun snowing again. The fur covers wrapped around his boots were plunging deeper into the snow with every step. The first flakes landed on his shoulder. There weren't many hours of daylight left, but Bashinoir still continued onwards.

If something happened to me, what would Lil and Miril do? I need to go back.

He decided that he'd head back as soon as the path veered in a different direction.

Once the path turned, he realized he was just a little ways away from one of his favorite spots. The trail climbed up a cliff a few hundred feet high. Bashinoir knew this was dangerous terrain. He thought about what would happen if he fell. He visualized himself at the bottom of the steep slope, with a wounded leg, unable to stand up. The snow would cover his footsteps. Lil and Miril wouldn't be able to find him, but if they kept looking, all that remained would be the frozen fragments of a cadaver mauled by wild animals.

He walked on a little further, feeling a shiver of danger, then, finally, decided to turn back. He went down to the forest, passed through it and reached the village, and then the Temple, without facing any problems during the return journey.

Approaching the Temple, he saw the light from the kitchen filtering through the windows. There was a hearth inside, a dinner and two women who, although tired from the work they had done that day, still wanted to spend time with him. Bashinoir wished he could just be alone, away from it all, even the woman he loved. He wished he could go straight to his bedroom, but didn't know how he could possibly do that. He had to save face, he had to pretend to be strong in front of those who had faith in him. He couldn't show them he was cracking. He felt overcome by nausea. What lie would he make up this time? What could he tell them about his day? Depressed, defeated, unable to break the spell that kept pulling him downwards, he stepped through the door, putting a spring in his step and a smile on his face.

32

While cleaning the large, round room of the Temple, Lil stopped to rest, wiping the sweat away from her forehead with a handkerchief. She allowed herself a few minutes to appreciate the marvelous mosaics decorating the walls. In the past, she, like all the other inhabitants of the island, would only have had the chance to spend time in this place while engaged in some humble form of work. It was one of the greatest honors one could aspire to. But now she was the only one left to take care of so many rooms. If she didn't finish cleaning before beginning the rituals, she would have to come back at night. It was inconceivable to leave any corner of the Temple in anything but the most perfect state of cleanliness.

Miril came into the room. Lil's heart ached when she saw her: they had woken up only a few hours ago, but Miril already looked like she was consumed with fatigue. Without saying a word, the priestess picked up a broom and began sweeping the floor.

"Priestess, please. You look exhausted. Let me take care of this," Lil said, coming closer and taking the broom handle away from her.

Her eyes were lined with dark, purple circles. The priestess smiled: "Don't worry. I'm happy to have something to do with my hands."

Lil replied with an insistence she swiftly regretted: "But why do you have to be so tired? I don't think you've slept in days!"

"There are lots of things I need to do. But your energy grows stronger every day, so soon I'll have the help I need."

"Priestess, I'm so sorry! I really wish I could do more right now. I can't bear seeing you so worn out."

"You're so sweet."

Miril hugged Lil, who placed her head on the woman's shoulder, breathing in the intense fragrance of her hair. The embrace was reassuring. When Lil lifted her head again, she looked the priestess in the eyes. Miril's gaze was gentle, Lil's was still slightly concerned.

The young woman became aware of a feeling she had never felt before. She was attracted to that face, to that woman, to that soul and to that energy. She felt herself getting lost in the kindness of her gaze. She closed her own eyes, as if she felt she couldn't handle such an intense emotion. An abnormal vibration traveled through her, and

Lil worried Miril would notice it. She wanted to move even closer to those lips, but she felt the woman's hands tense up.

What am I doing? Lil asked herself, opening her eyes. The priestess, frightened, was glaring at her as if she were a monster. Lil's heart started to race. *What did I do? Where did I go wrong?*

"I didn't...I...Forgive me. What did I do? I'm sorry! Forgive me, please, priestess," she babbled.

"No, no. Lil, you didn't do anything. It's just that, for a few seconds, I saw you *vanish.*"

"Vanish? What do you mean?"

"For a fraction of a second, your body appeared to become transparent!"

Oh, that poor woman, Lil sympathized. "Miril, I'm sorry. You're far too tired. You can't go on like this, you'll get sick," she said, almost whimpering, taking her hands. "Please, priestess, you need to rest."

"No, it's not because of fatigue. It's already happened once before, but at that time, we had spent so many hours performing the rituals that I thought it was just due to weakness. Besides, we weren't standing as close together then as we are now, so I really only noticed it out of the corner of my eye. But this time...this time you were right in front of me. And the walls of the Temple, the columns, the mosaics, nothing else lost its consistency. Only you."

"Miril, what are you saying? I didn't notice a thing. I didn't feel any drop in energy. Actually, when I closed my eyes, I felt warmth and...attraction," Lil admitted, looking at the floor.

"Lil, I know what I'm talking about. I need to go to the library and find an explanation for what just happened. And perhaps it'll also explain where the cadavers have all disappeared to."

33

"There is an ancient legend, an epic poem that tells of a people who go to a funeral, during which the body of the dead man disappears. Then, even the bodies of the living begin to experience flashes of transparency which, over the years, become increasingly frequent, until the people begin to vanish entirely. The poem ends with this sentence: *and the dry branch of time fell from the tree.*"

Bashinoir and Lil silently listened to the explanations of Miril, who had spent the entire day in the library, only emerging a few moments before dinner. She had told Lil what she had found out after so many hours of reading, and the young woman had begged her to also let Bashinoir participate in the discussion.

"I'm afraid," Miril continued, "that somehow the course of history has been changed, and that, now, we find ourselves on a dry branch."

Lil and Bashinoir struggled to wrap their minds around these ideas.

"This would explain why the cadavers disappeared. Since they have lower frequencies than living beings, they simply vanished, as on the new branch of time, they never existed. And, slowly, that's also what's happening to us. We're starting to disappear, because in theory, we've never existed."

Lil and Bashinoir involuntarily looked at one another, as if wanting to make sure they were both still present.

Bashinoir shyly allowed himself to comment: "I haven't noticed any *disappearing* going on here. Not even for a few seconds."

Miril tried to find the right words in order to avoid offending him. "At first only a well-trained eye is able to see it, but soon, the phenomenon becomes obvious to anyone and everyone."

Lil spoke up: "Priestess, could it perhaps be explained by the fact that, among the three of us, you're under the most stress? You carry the weight of the rituals almost entirely upon your own shoulders, since I'm still only able to do so little. Maybe -"

"Lil, believe me. I clearly saw what happened. And it's not because of fatigue. You were in front of me. Your face was a few inches away from mine and, through it, I saw the mosaics *behind* you. We can't attribute this simply to exhaustion."

Why were they so close to each other? Bashinoir wondered. An unpleasant sensation darted through him before he could repress it.

"Lil, Bashinoir, you have to imagine time not as a straight line leading from the past to the future, but as a living organism. Think of a plant – a bush, for example. There can be many temporal lines. But only one of them, only one particular branch, takes on the characteristics of reality."

"So what are the other branches, then?"

"They're possibilities. Events caused by other events which, however, don't have enough strength, or enough lymph, to transform into reality. At a certain point, these branches grow dry and fall off. And then only one temporal line is left."

"Then we should be on that line of time, right?" Lil asked.

"We were. I think that a new temporal line actually became stronger than our own. And on that new branch, our presence does not belong on this island, or we may not even exist at all, for that matter."

"I...I don't understand. How could things just change like this, all of a sudden?"

"It's hard to say for sure. We can only guess. I think that, in the past, a change was made so that our people never reached this island, in which case, we're no longer here," Miril explained, trying to find the simplest words that would be easier for them to understand.

Lil struggled to understand the complex matter at hand. Bashinoir wondered if Miril, due to all the stress she was under, was perhaps starting to lose it. "But what could have changed the past? Everything in the past has already happened. Nobody and nothing can do anything about it," he tried to object.

Miril thought for a moment. "That's not entirely true. Our sacred texts are rather clear in saying that it's possible to change the past."

"How in the world is that possible?" Lil objected, now alarmed.

"Through time travel."

"Time travel?" Bashinoir and Lil asked in unison.

They're not ready to understand. Maybe I shouldn't have even tried to explain this.

"Lil, Bashinoir: imagine that you're at a particular moment of the past. If you eliminate a future mother, she won't give birth to her baby, who won't be able to have their own children. With your action, you would have changed the course of time. Time would try

106

to reabsorb this change, but if that baby was destined to become a king or change the course of history, a new branch of time would probably have to develop. If the effects of temporal changes are too major to be reabsorbed, the new branch becomes stronger than the main branch, which then dries up and falls off."

"I don't understand!" Lil groaned. "Who could possibly go around making those sorts of changes?"

"Perhaps the same people responsible for the rock shards that rained down upon this island. Our rituals ensure the protection of the Temple and the island. Physically, nobody can hurt us, because we sustain a barrier that is impossible for them to get through. They could have, however, modified the past in order to give us the coup de grace, relying upon our inability to fight against their magical offense." *And they were probably right.*

34

Bashinoir wasn't convinced. He slept poorly, unable to rest: the words of priestess Miril continuously hammered through his dreams and thoughts all night long. Time travel, transparency, time as a living being, the dry branches: none of this made any sense. *Has the priestess gone crazy?*

For weeks, he had anxiously waited for her to provide an explanation for the deathly shower of rock shards and, finally, she came out with a theory as wacky as it was improbable.

Bashinoir was certain he hadn't noticed anything unusual about the consistency of their bodies. After that discussion, his doubts had not only remained unsolved, but now dominated everything else in his mind.

He had gotten up before dawn, eating a meager breakfast. On his way out, he hastily bade Lil and Miril good morning.

He naturally avoided the stables, where he should have performed the necessary work. He immediately chose the path that led through the woods, not without looking over his shoulder several times to make sure neither of the two women had come out of the Temple to get a breath of fresh air.

Once on the beach, Bashinoir enjoyed the morning sun for a few hours, trying in vain to erase the priestess's words from his mind.

He thought about the shadow. Whenever it came to keep him company, he always felt that he regained the peace and serenity he had lost, as if it recharged his energy needed to go onwards.

Their relationship was growing. The sensations were becoming increasingly palpable. *But it's a shadow that bobs around underwater!* Bashinoir was afraid it was just a product of his own mind. *What if it didn't exist? Maybe the only reason I see it is because I feel so lonely. There's nobody left, besides her.* Yet, after all the doubts raised by the conversation from the night before, he felt he desperately needed that contact tonight.

He walked along the beach, heading North. Although he was still several hundred feet away, he began to feel its presence. *This doesn't make sense. It's all a figment of my imagination. I'm deluding myself to think that this thing can communicate with me. It doesn't even exist.* Just coming closer to it, however, helped him feel better.

Once he reached their usual meeting place, he sat down on the beach, a few feet away from her. The sea was calm. Following the rhythm of the waves, the shadow rose and fell placidly.

Bashinoir closed his eyelids. Breaking through the crisp morning air, the sunshine warmed his face as the singing of the birds gently comforted him. The presence of the shadow was so allaying that it melted away his doubts, anxieties, tensions, and fears. Finally, he was at peace with himself.

Bashinoir, can you feel me?

Astonished, he opened his eyes again: only the shadow was there, in front of him, bobbing along with the water. In fact, he was sure that he hadn't heard anything, but that he had felt those words *inside* of him.

No, that's impossible! The desire to get up and walk away quickly overrode the confusion of emotions that washed through him. *It's nothing but an illusion!*

As he was about to stand back up, he noticed how low the sun still was on the horizon. *How am I going to spend the rest of the day?* The idea of going back to wander through the woods, at the mercy of all kinds of anxieties, didn't appeal to him. *Those words are just the product of my own mind. I'm okay here, there's nothing wrong.*

He again closed his eyes. A gust of icy wind blew against his face.

Don't be afraid.

He had heard it, this time there was no question about it. The three words had distinctly echoed through his head. He opened his eyes, looking around. He carefully observed the shadow. *I shouldn't be afraid?* The idea that it could not only transmit sensations, but now words, piqued his curiosity. He decided to close his eyes again and relax.

I'm here with you.

Fear and relief: someone or something was *communicating* with him. It was a shadow. Maybe it wasn't real, maybe it was just an illusion; but it would be so nice to finally be able to open his heart to another creature.

"Who are you?" he asked aloud. Talking to himself made him feel awkward, but a reply arose almost immediately in his mind.

I'm your friend.

"My friend?"

I sensed your suffering from very far away and I felt I couldn't just leave you alone.

Bashinoir's heart rejoiced. He continued repeating to himself that this was probably all in his head, that none of this was real, but he decided he couldn't just stop there, whether or not it was an illusion.

"Well, you got that right. I feel very alone. Terrible things have happened on this island."

I'm only able to sense your presence.

"Here, right now, it's just me, but really I live with two women, who are almost always in the Temple. I'm the only person who can go out around the island."

Why are there only three of you?

"Everyone else who lived on this island is now...dead."

The shadow, kindly and tactfully, continued to ask him all sorts of questions, which Bashinoir, eager to confide in someone, readily answered.

Towards the end of one of his explanations, Bashinoir paused, uncertain of what to say next.

What is it? What's bothering you?

"Well, last night, the priestess told us some of her hypotheses. They were rather odd. She thinks..." and Bashinoir recounted what he had retained after hearing Miril's theories.

I'm sorry but I have to go now. I'll come back to see you soon, but I can't stay now.

"Wait! Tell me what you are!"

I will. Later. I promise. I'll be back soon and I'll answer any questions you have for me. See you then.

Bashinoir stared as the shadow darted away through the water.

35

Gazing at herself in the mirror, Aleia delighted in how beautiful she looked. She carefully examined every corner of her face, looking for changes or signs of aging. It seemed as if any potential wrinkles were under control, thanks in part to the herbal wraps the masters prepared for her. Satisfied, she smiled at her reflection, while the brush, moved by Nuris' expert hand, trailed through her auburn hair.

She looked up at the young woman, one of the many wives of Beanor who took turns waiting on her. There was only one woman in the palace who had the privilege of being served by the other wives. And that was her. The others had to content themselves with regular servants. Such an arrangement had made it very clear to the other wives that they were to defer to her, whenever they found themselves in her presence.

Her hair was perfect: soft, long, vividly red, just how the monarch liked it. There was a time when all it took was a slight movement of that mane to capture every speck of the king's attention and bewitch his body, after which he would fall helplessly at her feet. There was a time...before Beanor's bedroom was regularly invaded by younger consorts, women whom she herself had to teach to conform to all of the royal preferences and requirements. *Almost all of them*, she smiled to herself. There were a few secrets she kept to herself, as she would remain the only woman able to fulfill *every* one of his desires.

Zilia, another wife, was meticulously following the instructions Aleia had given her for her makeup. Two shadows trailed from the end of Aleia's eyes which, from the black of her eyelashes, blended into a scarlet red that tapered gradually towards her temples. No other wife in the palace was able to pull off such sophisticated makeup or, perhaps, none other dared to challenge her in this field. In either case, the latest proof of her supremacy pleased her immensely.

Aleia adjusted her bosom, pushing her breasts up towards the generous neckline that framed them.

Her long dress, a dark red color with black embroidery, perfectly matched the colors of her makeup and hair. No wardrobe, not even that of her crude husband, was comparable to hers.

Aleia was absolutely satisfied with her morning preparations. Zilia and Nuris had perfectly fulfilled their duties. During the day, she would reward them with special kindness.

Towards them, as towards any other wife, Aleia felt not just the simple desire to dominate them, but also an acute sense of duty and responsibility. Without the hierarchy she imposed upon them, with her rules and through her command, chaos would have broken out among the king's wives, and he would not have been the least bit pleased with that.

"You may go," she told the two consorts, giving them a polite smile.

Before the door closed completely, Aleia assigned them one last task: "Oh...and send me the new girl. That maid."

Although the king promoted women from the most disparate social classes to the rank of wife, this didn't mean that the first wife had any respect for them. As long as the new wife remained a regular underneath the royal sheets, she would find it difficult to gain acceptance from the other consorts. When the king, however, felt the need to switch his focus to another from his harem, the latest arrival, already in a tenuous position, would timidly begin to reach out and establish contact with the others. But only Aleia had the power to decide when she could truly come out of isolation. No spouse would have dared to extend a friendly welcome to any woman who the first wife had not yet officially accepted.

A knock on the door, followed by a request in an unusually high and confident voice, distracted her from her thoughts: "May I come in?"

"Of course! Please, make yourself comfortable!" Aleia invited her, leaving her dressing table and heading to the parlor.

Milia sat in front of her, looking her brazenly in the eye. Her smooth, blonde hair fell down to her shoulders. Her eyes were a dense, direct blue that candidly burst forth. She sat up straight, her legs together, her hands resting on her knees, her young and slender arms closed in a white tunic.

Aleia hated that impudent presence. Smiling cordially, she rang a little bell. Milia instinctively moved, as if she wanted to run away. Aleia acknowledged the young woman's involuntary reaction with a smug smile. As soon as a hidden door behind a column opened, Aleia commented: "Oh, here's my *servant*."

She ordered an herbal tea for both of them, without asking the girl which flavor she preferred. In the blink of an eye, the servant came back with the steaming beverages. Aleia waited until she was alone with the young wife before breaking the silence. She took a certain pleasure in the awkward pause, even if the girl's cheeky stare led her to believe there was much work to be done.

"So, Milia. I imagine it's a nice change of pace to sit comfortably while someone else serves you something to drink," she provoked her, sipping from her cup.

"Not quite, my lady. Despite my new position, I'm still forced to do what others tell me to do. You know I didn't come here by my own choice."

What a personality this one has! "Yes, well, pleasing our king in bed is certainly not the same thing as cleaning the houses of other people."

Milia looked away, and Aleia noticed a hint of deep sorrow.

"Before...I had hope," she confessed absentmindedly.

So that's what it's about! "Oh, I understand. Listen girl, whatever that little hope was about, you'd be best to forget about it now that you're here. If the king ever becomes the slightest bit suspicious that you're not fully concentrated on your duties, and should he then find out why, the only thing you'll be able to hope for is death or escape. And, as you may already know, around here those two things are one and the same."

A tear fell down the fair skin of Milia's face.

"Oh, come on! He's your king, after all. Don't think you're the first to leave a broken heart in your wake. Why worry about a few hateful stares directed towards the royal apartments from the hovels below?"

Milia answered by glaring at her, full of rage and obstinacy.

At least she managed to stop crying. She must think she's better than all of us. Let's see if that proves to be true!

"Milia, over time, you'll come to understand that although things around the palace might seem a little *strange*, it's so much nicer to live here than anywhere else outside of these walls. And – oh, silly me! I forgot my shawl on my bed. Would you please go get it for me?"

Milia nodded and got up, then paused. She glanced over at the bed, at the end of which laid the black garment the woman had asked

113

her for.

She gave her an annoyed look, to which Aleia responded with a wide smile. Milia finally got up and strode over to retrieve the shawl, then dropped it brusquely into Aleia's lap. The first wife thanked her politely.

"You'll find out that being the king's wife entails a few responsibilities, as well as a world of pleasure. It's up to you to figure out how to behave, what to pay attention to, and how to best enjoy what your enviable position can offer."

Rather than reply, Milia stared out the window, distracted, although Aleia didn't quite understand that was an expression of indifference.

"I don't think I slept well at all last night. Would you be so kind as to relieve my shoulders with a nice little massage from your young little hands?"

Milia looked at her, perplexed. "What hurts?"

"Just a little pain here." She pointed to the top of her right shoulder.

"Maybe a healer would be better for that, don't you think?" Milia retorted.

"Oh no, I don't like them very much. And besides, I'm absolutely curious to discover the charms hidden within the touch of your hands."

Milia, with a slight snort, stood up and walked behind Aleia, a grim expression spreading over her face.

Much to Aleia's surprise, Milia began massaging her with extraordinary grace. Her fingertips dove down to the right spot with a firm, yet elegant, movement. Although she didn't really have any pains that needed to be tended to, she felt extremely pleasant sensations.

Milia's hands traveled up Aleia's neck, alternating gentle touches from her fingertips with pressure of varying intensity, even using her palms and her elbows.

Aleia was in ecstasy. She closed her eyes, letting herself get carried away with those superb caresses and, without realizing it, moaned with pleasure until the pressure, after slowly decreasing, finally came to a complete stop.

The woman opened her eyes, coming back down to earth. She realized Milia was still behind her. *Why did she stop?* She loved being massaged. "Everything alright, Milia?"

"Yes, of course. And you, do you feel better?"

"Oh...you have such a *divine* touch. I imagine you've gotten a lot of practice in the past. Are you tired?"

"I get the impression that your pain has gone away."

"Indeed, it's almost all gone. However, I'm sure that if you continued, you'd help prevent it from coming back in the future."

Milia walked confidently in front of the first wife, her eyes furious, her arms crossed. "Pardon me. I'm well aware of your position in the palace. Recall, however, that now *I*, too, am one of the king's wives. And I would appreciate it if you didn't confuse me with one of your maids."

Aleia, witnessing the young woman's outburst, felt a secret sense of victory. It had taken so little to get that sort of reaction out of her. *Alright, we shall do what must be done. Allow me to take the opportunity to teach this little tart how things work around her.* Bending, molding, educating the wives, granting every one of them the position she deserved, governing over them: this was the real work of the true queen of the palace.

"My dear, young wife of our beloved king Beanor, ruler of Isk, perhaps you still haven't realized that it is *I* who governs the royal palace. This is my domain. You do what I tell you to do. I make every decision regarding everything within these walls: from receptions to kitchens, from parties to ceremonies, from governing the king's young wives to everything that concerns his pleasure. I decide, I arrange, I decree, and I administer. It's a duty that I would happily go without, but I know that I have to do it in order to relieve the king from concerns that are not worthy of his attention."

She wasn't asking any questions. She could have been more subtle, but she rarely found herself in the presence of such a rebellious creature. Perhaps transforming from servant girl to the king's favorite toy had already gone to the impudent maid's head.

Milia didn't let up: "I'm happy that you do so much for our own good, but I'd like to remind you that I'm the one who sleeps under the royal sheets now. And the king seems to have a character that is, all in all, very easy to influence when requests are made at particularly strategic moments of intimate encounters."

The girl seems to have understood quite a bit in just a short time.

"And so?" the first wife asked, provocatively.

"And so I don't want to be another one of your slaves, since you already have plenty, official and otherwise!"

Aleia smiled. It had been a while since she found herself in such a situation. Finally, an amusing diversion, a task that would be especially satisfying to fulfill.

As she opened her mouth to speak, the door suddenly flew open. King Beanor, his chest bare, wearing only pants and boots, burst into the room: "Aleia, please, remind me what type of – oh!" he exclaimed, realizing Milia was there. "Your servant told me you were here. I didn't realize you had company. Well, I'm delighted that you're getting to know one another," he commented, intrigued to see his first wife sitting comfortably and his new wife standing, her arms crossed, in front of her, with an expression that didn't seem all that pleasant.

Milia answered with a low curtsy as Aleia kept her seat: "Your Majesty, I believe I've asked you for several decades now to kindly knock before rudely barging into my bedroom."

Beanor, confused and wary, understood something wasn't right: "Yes, that's true."

"Now, your young wife was actually demonstrating just how skilled a masseuse she is. She really does have a magic touch! We were working on her technique so that, one of these evenings, she might be good enough for the royal appendages."

A few provocative images flashed through Beanor's mind, exciting him immediately as his member began to rise. He had come in at just the right time. His eyes shone with an immoderate interest: "Excellent. That sounds like a fine idea to me."

"Absolutely, your Majesty. Milia has an uncanny talent, something we have never before seen in this palace."

Aleia, aware that she had the king's entire attention, smiled, satisfied.

Beanor was already ravenous. He wondered if it would be possible to call the advisor and postpone the imminent formal engagements. "I want to try it right away!"

"Oh no," Aleia retorted. "The girl isn't ready yet. We need to refine her technique. After working through her shoulder technique, we were going to start on the foot massage."

"Actually, your Highness, I believe I'm already prepared to devote myself to you," Milia butted in.

Beanor looked at his first wife: calm, relaxed, smiling, sure of herself. The expression of the other woman, however, was incomprehensible to him, but he knew that younger women were always a little moody. In any case, Aleia never made mistakes and, if she thought there was still a need to refine her technique, then Beanor had no desire to contradict her.

The king's mind wandered off through images of pure delight. He didn't know what he'd do without that woman, Aleia. In theory, she was only a wife, and had been for a long time. Many others had charms, or beauty, or young bodies that she no longer had, but she possessed something none of the others had, and Beanor was well aware that without the perverse preparations of Aleia, it would take weeks, if not months, to ensure the education of the young wives himself. But he was impatient by nature and Aleia, despite everything, was able to give him exactly what he wanted within the right amount of time. Moreover, because of her, he didn't have to worry about little details. Yes, Aleia was a true queen, and if she asked for privileges that were not theoretically hers in return, he was fine with that. As it was, in some cases, he was more than happy with that.

"His Majesty's appendages," the first wife continued, "are very precious and sensitive. You're lucky to be able to practice on me: when it's time for you to gladden him with these splendid massages, my corrections will help you to avoid exerting pressure which, from time to time, still feels somewhat rough. Sire, watch with your own eyes what an enthusiastic student Milia is."

Aleia's eyes moved from the king's face to the face of the young wife. With the eldest wife's eyelids slightly closed, her makeup gave her an even more wicked expression, as the pupils, shining through the slits, appeared to feed off the emotions of the girl standing before her.

"Come forward, Milia. Give our king a little demonstration of your graces. Please, continue. Don't be shy – you can massage me in front of His Majesty, even if there are some other matters best kept between women, not at all appropriate for his ears."

A raging glare in Milia's eyes ignited, then immediately disappeared. She knelt down at the feet of the first wife, who was still wearing her black open flats with leather laces that climbed up over her ankles.

Milia subserviently undid the knot and slid down the laces, removing the shoe from the queen's foot.

Aleia thoroughly enjoyed reminding the girl of her servant status, in front of the king, at that. Her eyes freely expressed the emotions she felt in that moment.

Beanor was deeply conflicted. Merely the image of those two splendid women, one fascinating and intriguing, the other young and gorgeous, one at the feet of the other, was making him forget about his official engagements. In the end, he was the king, and it was right that he enjoyed the pleasures reserved for his position every once in a while.

His erection was so hard that it hurt as it pressed against his pants. He noticed how his first wife looked at it, pleased, out of the corner of her eyes, and he took a few steps towards the two women, openly stroking himself. Milia, who had been massaging the queen's feet with great care and attention, looked up, surprised.

After dawdling a little, Beanor started to undo his pants, but a knock at the door broke the spell the king had been under.

It was Tuirl: "Your Majesty, our guests have requested your presence. They've already been waiting quite a long time."

Beanor greedily looked at his two wives and admonished them, unable to take his eyes off that splendid vision: "Continue your lesson. As soon as I come back, ladies, I want to find you exactly how I left you."

Victory! Aleia imagined the king coming back to find the servant already dead tired, incapable of the vigorous physical activity that could only satisfy the king's desires. She, on the other hand, after that long, relaxing massage, would be happy to show Beanor once again that no wife compared to her.

36

The priestess Miril stood in the doorway of the Temple. The enormous, dark wooden doors loomed over her slender silhouette. The cold air rushed into the foyer like an army hellbent on conquering new territory. Miril, covered by her light azure robe, her hair woven in a chestnut braid that trailed down her back, didn't seem to notice.

Lil walked past the atrium, heading towards the rooms tucked deep inside the Temple, where she would begin the ritual preparations.

"Come here," Miril invited her, without turning around.

Lil joined her on the doorstep.

"It's such a beautiful day. How unfortunate that we're unable to take a pleasant stroll together through the woods!" the priestess said. Lil detected a mixture of hope and sadness in her voice, but didn't reply.

"But now we must leave. I'm afraid it's the only solution."

The priestess's words shocked Lil.

"Miril, where do you want to go?"

"To wherever the new branch of time was created."

Lil still didn't understand the strange theory about branches of time, nor had she noticed any of the transparent visions Miril had reported. Yet she couldn't deny the fact that it was hard to explain why the dead bodies had disappeared. She still had an unshakable faith in the woman who guided her, although all this talk of time travel seemed equally absurd and impossible to her. "Miril, do you think that's possible?" she asked politely.

"Our ancestors left us a few scrolls that could provide some useful indications. It'll take a lot of preparation, and we're not guaranteed to finish the process in time, but I spent all last night trying to think up an alternative solution and, quite honestly, I don't think there are any."

A plethora of questions flooded through Lil's mind. There was so much she wanted to know, she couldn't decide what to ask first. She forgot all about the cold air blowing in her face. Instead, her racing heartbeat overwhelmed her, warming her from inside.

"And once we're there, what will we do?"

"I don't really know, Lil. We have no idea who created the new branch of time, not to mention why they did it. We can assume it was the same person who called forth the shower of stone shards. But until we have some proof, there's little else we can know for sure."

"But Miril, what will happen to the Temple while we're gone?"

She smiled: "Nothing. As long as we manage to come back, we'll only be gone for a moment or two. From what I've read, if we use the right magical techniques, we can plan the trip so that we leave and come back within the same minute."

Lil felt her heart was going to jump outside of her chest. She was incredibly frightened. "And what if we don't come back? What if something happens?"

The priestess lifted her hand to the young woman's face and caressed it gently. "Lil, what will happen to us if we don't at least try this final, however extreme, option? Waiting would be riskier than taking action."

"Yes, but..." Lil wanted to confess that, deep down, she wasn't sure of Miril's explanations, but she didn't have the courage to say so.

"Yes, I'm certain what I told you is true," Miril responded to Lil's unexpressed thoughts.

I need to practice shielding my thoughts, Lil reflected.

Come here, Miril urged her, hugging her. "We'll make it, you'll see," she whispered.

Out of the corner of her eye, she noticed a movement at the edge of the forest. She turned around to get a better look, but didn't notice anything out of the ordinary. The same thought came to both of their minds at the same time.

Miril was brave enough to bring up the subject: "Yes, I think he should come with us."

Bashinoir didn't seem to have fully recovered after the massacre. Perhaps spending so much time alone, with difficult tasks to perform, was simply too much for him. Lil felt he was growing more distant, more defeated every day, but she was convinced he just needed time to accept such a massive loss, not to mention the loss of his wife's company. Sometimes she was tempted to delve more deeply into his worries, to sort through his thoughts, but her ethics prevented her from doing so. Telepathy was traditionally allowed

120

among the priest class, as all of the members had to act with a single mind. Beyond that, the ancestors had established limits, out of respect for privacy. Lil was still concerned and even hurt by her husband's distance. He had built an insurmountable wall, behind which he hid from her and the priestess.

Miril continued: "We can't ask him to stay here alone, nor can we just leave without saying a word. If we don't come back, it would be far too cruel to have disappeared without telling him anything. We really don't know what we're going to find, and the support of a man could be crucial."

Lil could hardly fathom the idea of leaving the island where she had always lived, much less traveling to another time entirely. The unknown, the danger, the theory of the branches of time: everything whirled around her mind as total confusion set in. But one question in particular weighed upon her heart: "Miril, do you know where to go?"

The priestess smiled at her, even more tenderly than usual. "No. We'll have to figure that out together. From what I've read, this requires a very long and complicated process of intense preparation. I have no idea how we'll be able to continue with the rituals, your training, and this new task, all at the same time. I'm afraid we'll often have to work through most of the night, and this may very well weaken our ability to concentrate.

"Now, there are magical techniques we can use to climb up our branch of time until we reach the point where we sense the divergence from the new branch. In that spot, the frequencies should be different. We'll have to use the techniques described in the ancient texts to figure out the appropriate solution. It'll be like traveling up a river, looking for a tributary with a different color of water – a different color that comes from flowing over a different type of earth.

"The same idea applies to finding the place. Imagine throwing a stone into a pond. The ripples will move away from where the object touched the water. Studying the wrinkles in time, we'll be able to identify the point where the stone landed, the beginning of the new branch. And once we get those coordinates, we'll travel in that direction."

Lil was upset. After the rock shards had come plunging down from the sky, the only solace she had found was staying within the reassuring walls of the Temple, a comfort now threatened by the priestess's proposal. She was afraid she didn't have the strength nor the skills to perform a task so far beyond the limits of her imagination.

"We'll stay together, don't worry," Miril promised her sweetly, but this time, not even her telepathic sensitivity could soothe her.

"Miril, couldn't we just go alone and see what happens, then come back here and decide what to do?" Lil surprised herself with her own words. But it seemed right to be more cautious, given how delicate the situation was.

Miril, her eyes hopeful yet veiled with sadness, replied: "After looking through the sacred books, I went to the laboratory to see what elements we have available. I found some ancient urns that seem to contain the necessary materials, materials I don't think came from this island. Our ancestors probably brought them from the Northern lands. I did a quick calculation of how much we would need and, unfortunately, we only have enough material for a very limited number of trips through time."

"And how many would that be?" Lil asked, terrified of the response.

"Only two. There and back."

37

Bashinoir was annoyed. The night before, Lil and Miril had tormented him by asking lots of questions about what he had been doing lately, particularly what parts of the island he had visited and how far along he was in transferring the animals to the stables close to the Temple. Despite his reluctance to answer, and although they still continued with their questions, they remained kind and understanding, treating him as a problematic child who, for whatever reason, could not be scolded. To him, that false and condescending attitude was really intolerable. If they were mad at him for some reason, it would be better that they expressed it openly.

Did they find out? Considering they never leave the Temple, how would they know anything?

That day, he decided to go back to his old house, the little cottage where he and Lil had lived while waiting to build their new house. He lit a fire, took off his boots and comfortably settled into the rocking chair near the hearth. Opposite the fireplace, on the other side of the small yet cozy room, was the stove Lil used to cook over. A large table stood in the center. A staircase led to the little attic where their bed was. It hadn't been damaged badly by the shards of stone: there were only a few small holes that could be easily repaired.

Their bed. Just remembering it made him feel a deep pang of nostalgia for the nights they had kept each other warm, the nights when he enjoyed the sweet smell of his wife.

But now Lil was far away from him. She seemed even more beautiful and unobtainable, splendid as she shone in a new light, more alive than the flames that danced in front of him, her eyes as bright as two suns. There didn't seem to be any room for him in her new life. They hardly spent any time together during the day; and the priestess Miril was always around. Not only did the two women work together, but they had built up an unusually strong trust he felt excluded from. And what about him? The few times they had found themselves alone, just Lil and him, Bashinoir had wanted to laugh and joke around the way he used to, but he didn't feel good enough for her anymore and had assumed she wouldn't find his jovial remarks very funny.

Bashinoir would have given anything to feel his wife's eyes, full of desire, look at him how they used to, when she pretended like she wanted to run away, anxious for him to prove his manhood as he chased after her.

He closed his eyes, enjoying the crackling of the small fire in his ears and the heat of the flame that warmed his body and face.

He imagined his wife running out of the Temple and playing hide and go seek with him.

He rubbed one hand over his pants.

Lil kept running, turning around only to give him a naughty smile.

Bashinoir opened his fly and held his member in his right hand, stroking it.

Lil was hiding behind a corner, but when Bashinoir thought he had finally caught up with her, she had already disappeared. He looked around. A noise came from the spot where his wife was hiding. He anticipated her movements, heading towards a place where he would be able to cut off her escape.

His fingers firmly gripped his member as they rose and fell. *It's been so long since I've had this kind of pleasure!*

Bashinoir went and hid behind a wall. He heard Lil's footsteps as she walked, looking behind her shoulder. Without realizing it, she ended up right in his arms.

That sudden contact excited him immensely. His hand started to move more quickly. His breath accelerated.

Lil looked at him, helpless, her eyes begging him to set her free. He loved that look.

His hand accelerated.

He grabbed both of her wrists as his lips came down upon hers. Lil pretended to resist, then opened her mouth, letting his tongue enter. But suddenly Lil stepped back: "No! I'm a novice!"

Bashinoir felt horrible. Abusing a novice was one of the worst crimes imaginable. Yet Lil was so seductive. And their people were gone. It was only the two of them now.

His hand stopped moving. Had he just allowed himself to imagine taking a novice?

She used to be his wife, though.

He closed his eyes again as his hand resumed its movement.

Lil resisted. A girl in her position wouldn't give in easily, so

124

Bashinoir took her in his arms and brought her to the bed in their room as she squirmed and kicked, unable to overcome his physical prowess. When he laid her upon the bed, she wriggled as if to escape, but her eyes betrayed a desire even stronger than his own.

"No, Bashinoir! You know I can't!" Lil scolded him, her voice teasing, her eyes mischievous.

Instead of answering, Bashinoir opened his pants, lifted up her dress and laid his body over hers. She squeezed her legs shut in resistance. Jutting his pelvis down, however, he was able to open her legs. He pushed in and penetrated her deeply.

At that thought, Bashinoir's hand moved in a fury, as if possessed. His penis was as hard as a rock and burned like the fire in the hearth.

Bashinoir moved in and out of her, matching the rhythm of his hand. Lil moaned, wet and excited, her eyes burning. Bashinoir possessed her as a real man would, letting all of his pleasure explode inside of her. Now she'd finally get pregnant, he hoped, and then there'd be at least one part of her husband she could never refuse. The image of his semen traveling through her excited him so much that Bashinoir's body stiffened, his hand finished a few final pumps and slowed down, just before he orgasmed. The image of his wife's sex, flooded with his semen, lingered in his mind.

At the peak of excitement, his hand lingered. Lowering it one last time, he ejaculated so forcefully that he squirted all over his shirt, up to his neck.

"That's for you, Lil," Bashinoir announced, proud to dedicate such a beautiful moment of self-pleasure to the sensual beauty of his former wife.

He laid still, enjoying the sensation for a little while.

The fire had grown weak. His penis, covered with semen, and the stains on his clothes started to make him feel uncomfortable. He got up and looked for something he could clean himself with. He took an old rag and wiped off his clothes.

He finally left the house. He had enjoyed that delightful moment in his old home, and promised himself to come back soon. But what should he do now? He could start working, although it really wouldn't make much of a difference if he decided to wait one more day. He was in a better mood than usual, and it would be nice to maintain it. More than anything else he needed a little social contact, so he decided to go to where he was almost sure he'd find his friend, the shadow.

38

So you two were able to save yourselves?

The setting sun illuminated the sky behind Bashinoir, who sullenly observed the shadow floating underneath the water in front of him. Their conversation was making him feel uncomfortable.

"Yes, we managed to survive. I think it was a miracle. The rock shards were falling everywhere. Looking back, I still can't believe they didn't hit us. I only got one little wound on my calf."

Bashinoir stared out over the sea, observing how it grew darker in the distance. He took in a deep breath.

And the priestess? She managed to stay out of harm's way?

"She was in the Temple when everything happened."

But didn't you tell me that everyone, even the priests, participated in the important rituals?

"I don't really know why she wasn't there. But I think it's just our tradition. It's normal for only one priest to be with us, while the other stays in the Temple."

For the magical protections, right?

"Sure. I mean, to maintain the magical forces of the island, otherwise we'd be in danger. I don't understand much about it though. Us regular folks only know what the elders tell us about it."

So the priestess was the one taking care of all of the magical protections at that moment?

"Yes. The priest was officiating the rites of union for the bride and groom."

So she was protecting the island during the rites?

A sinister doubt came over Bashinoir. He wanted to raise his voice, but he feared losing the only friend he still had. He would have walked away, but then he'd have to think of something else to do for the rest of the afternoon. It was still too early to make an appearance back at the Temple.

"I don't know! We don't know anything about magical protections. We only know that the priests are the people who take care of those things!"

Of course, of course. Has something like this ever happened in the past?

Bashinoir's eyes followed the hypnotic movements of the shadow underneath the water. He dug his fingers into the cold sand, snorting.

"Why are you asking me all of these questions?"

Pardon me. I live alone and nobody's ever told me anything about temples, priests or magic before. But we can change the subject if you'd like. It's just that I'm a bit worried.

"Why?"

What if you're in danger? What if something happened to you? What would I do without you?

And what would I do without you? Bashinoir wondered. For a moment he forgot that the shadow could read his mind.

Our friendship is such a beautiful thing to me. I don't ever want to lose you.

"I don't want to lose you either. But I don't understand. Why are you worried about me being in danger? Do you think that what happened could happen again?"

No. Well, I mean, it depends...

"On what?"

See, that's what I don't understand! If your priests are so powerful, and one of them was even in the Temple protecting you, how could something like that happen without her even knowing about it?

That question hit Bashinoir like a punch in the stomach. He'd always had the feeling that something had gone terribly wrong on that cursed day and, deep down inside, he'd even started to resent the priestess. But he would never have dared to explicitly accuse her.

"You think she knew?"

I don't know. I have no way of knowing these things. But you told me before that the magical defenses have always been impenetrable. And it's strange that she didn't seem to be able to predict what was going to happen. Wouldn't a priest have been able to sense this sort of thing beforehand?

Bashinoir didn't have an answer. But he intuited that the shadow could be right.

Maybe afterwards, then, the priestess explained to you what had happened?

"Well, yes, she talked about the magical war with our enemies, about the subject of time..."

Did she explain why she wasn't able to warn you?

"No, she didn't."

Hmm. This is all so strange. Maybe she didn't know it was going to happen. Or maybe she did know and just didn't want to tell you.

"But that makes no sense!"

Yes, you're right. Why would a priestess ever want to kill her own people? But now what does she want to do?

"She says we also need to travel through time. She said the only way to repair this messed-up reality is to go back in time."

So she wants to leave the island?

"Yes, but we'll come back."

Ah ha! That's it!

Bashinoir felt increasingly conflicted. He didn't need to formulate any thoughts, since the shadow could feel his emotions, and a particularly painful suspicion circled through his mind: *Do you think she did all this just to get off the island?*

I have no idea. I only know what you tell me. But who wouldn't want to spend their future far away from a frozen, isolated island, where you have to spend day and night doing nothing but magical rituals, without the warmth of another human being next to you?

"Lil!" Bashinoir bellowed, distraught.

That's what I was thinking too, but I didn't want to make you worry.

Bashinoir was beside himself with anger. All the pieces of the puzzle now fit together. Why hadn't Miril protected them? Why didn't she even warn them about what was going to happen? Why did she steal his wife away from him?

"But then why did she ask me to travel through time with her?"

Maybe she doesn't actually want to travel through time. Maybe she just wants to travel through space, to find a nicer place to live. Once the transport ritual has been completed, she'd be the one to decide what happens next. If she told your wife she'd rather leave you here, Lil wouldn't agree to it at all. So she's just acting like she wants to do the right thing. But there's no guarantee that all three of you would get to the same destination.

Bashinoir was livid. *If that's what she's planning...*He clenched his fists and stood up. He was going to set things right, once and for all.

Where are you going? Stop!

"Why?"

Don't hurt her, you don't have any proof that any of this is true.

129

Besides, you need to be careful. She could start to use her magical powers against you. She's a priestess, she would surely win.

"So now what?" asked Bashinoir, rabid. "What should I do?"

You need to wait for the right moment.

39

Milia was on top of him, but she wasn't moving with her usual intensity. Just last night, that girl had driven him out of his mind. Yet now, this goddess of sex seemed to be out of it. After he orgasmed, she laid down beside him, her back to him, without doting on him as she usually did.

Beanor was enraged. Generally he would resolve this sort of problem by sending the girl out and calling in another one. But he still needed Milia. He was caught up in an unbridled passion, victim to a blind and inexhaustible desire that drove him to seek out the pleasures of her body every hour of the day.

She remained silent. He didn't know what to do. He wondered if he should ask her if something was wrong, but he had never been interested in the feelings of any of his subjects, even his wives.

They spent a few moments in awkward silence. Finally Beanor decided to approach the subject: "The weather these days is really making the ladies tired."

No response.

That lack of respect humiliated him. He instinctively searched the room for his sword, which he usually liked to use to resolve such situations. But it wasn't the right time, not yet. He was sure he'd never find such a gorgeous body and fleshy rump anywhere else in the kingdom.

"I'm your wife. I'm nobody's slave!"

Beanor's jaw dropped. Nobody had ever dared to speak to the king in that manner.

His hands itched, yet he couldn't forget what he had experienced over the past few nights. No, he needed to stay calm. He didn't want to forgo the embraces that had made him feel things he had never felt before.

"What are you trying to say? The only person you have to serve is me!"

"I don't think that's really how it works."

Arrogant, contrarian...How dare she? This haughty girl needs to be put back in her place!

Beanor was ready to make her understand the weight of his authority, but she turned around, tears streaming down her cheeks, and kissed him passionately. Then, her face barely an inch away from his, she told him: "Your Majesty, please, don't let me be a victim of that bully. I'll give you every pleasure in this world. You haven't seen anything yet, I've just begun to share my delights with you. But please, protect my days and I swear that your nights will be unforgettable!"

Beanor, caught by surprise, remained silent. He tried to think of who Milia could be referring to, but nobody came to mind.

He had no royal interest in the dissatisfactions of young women, but those tempting promises made him continue on: "Who dares to bother you during the day?"

"I think you know perfectly well who, your Majesty."

Impudent! Never before in so many years had he found himself in front of such a shameless hussy.

"You nasty little -" he started to say, a rage coming over him.

But she kissed him even more passionately. She placed a hand on his member and started to move it down with an unbearably slowness, lowering her head to stare at it while continuing to stroke him. "Your Majesty, please, don't be mean to me. I need your help."

"Carry on!" he ordered.

"Will you help me?" the girl asked, her movements still not accelerating.

"We'll talk about it later! Now get to work!" Beanor replied drily.

"No. I need to be reassured."

Beanor's eyes burned: "Fine! Tell me what's bothering you!"

40

Nal casually glances at her little brother. He hates subterfuge. He hasn't noticed anything yet. He's completely absorbed in his work. He fulfills the requirements for the magical protections, and once again looks over everything he needs to keep safe. She knows he'll discover her move soon enough, but only after it's too late. He'll get angry. But that's how you learn.

41

Unable to sleep, Lil tossed and turned in bed. The idea of time travel continued to torment her. The island had always been her horizon. Beaches and reefs were the borders of her universe. Rarely had she even gone out to sea with a fisherman. Only a few times had she dreamt of faraway lands, warm places she had heard about in fairytales, inhabited by people of all races wearing different colors of clothes.

But the thought of going back to the *past* terrorized her. They would have to visit a time when most of their people had been exterminated, the survivors forced to escape by sea. There were so many unknowns. Perhaps they, too, would get caught up in the massacre. Maybe they wouldn't be able to come back and would stay, trapped in a time full of turmoil and hardship. They could even get killed.

She trusted Miril, but her theories on the branches of time were almost impossible to grasp. She wondered if Miril was fully aware of what she was doing, but she didn't want to doubt her wisdom.

And then there was Bashinoir, increasingly distant and lost in his own world. The more she tried to get closer to him, the further he pulled away. He wasn't the same man she used to know. The situation hardly created the ideal conditions for taking this kind of trip. In any case, he had to come with them, they needed his strength. Who knows what they'd come up against. It would be almost impossible to work in three; in two, however, it was unthinkable.

She had lost almost everyone and everything in her life, and now, the little that remained, reconstructed with so much difficulty, was again about to slip away from her grasp.

"Lil." Miril called quietly, from the other side of the door.

"Yes?"

"You can't sleep, can you?"

"No."

"Neither can I."

Lil got up. Walking across the cold floor, she hurried to open the door and invited Miril in.

Miril was wearing a gauzy white dressing gown. She entered, passing the crackling fire which lit the room up with warm colors, spreading a pleasant warmth throughout the room. She knew how much Lil hated the cold.

Though she was very tired, Miril appeared to be as lucid as ever, unlike Lil, who felt discombobulated all the time.

Smiling, Miril sat on the edge of the bed. Lil imitated her.

"I know you never expected to be put to such a difficult test. You're afraid, and it's right that you should be. I, too, am terrified. Believe me, if there was another way, I'd be happy to avoid such a risky voyage. But unfortunately there is no other way, or at least, no other way I can think of. Despite all of the dangers that lie ahead, we have to leave. Our understanding of magic will help whenever our experience fails us."

The calm, sedate tone of voice filled the young woman's troubled mind with a sense of serenity.

"Lil, I want to tell you something." Miril paused, staring at the fire.

Her uncertainty rekindled Lil's own anxiety from a few moments earlier.

"We've overcome, and we're still facing some very difficult trials. What happened on our island is horrific, and you can't imagine how much I regret not having predicted what happened, and not setting up the right defenses. At any rate," again a long pause, "at any rate, during the course of this tragedy, I discovered something I never would have suspected. A beautiful feeling that helped me to salvage the tiniest bit of happiness."

Lil was curious. She realized her heart was racing. A crazy idea, immediately repressed by her own shame, flashed through her mind.

Miril let out a little sigh. Lil blushed.

"It's been really nice, spending these past few weeks with you," Miril said, timid, yet her words flowing out quickly, as if she wanted to relieve herself of a weight.

Lil was shocked. Those words didn't bother her, but suddenly everything seemed upside-down.

"Sorry," Miril said, confused. "I know that you've been married to him for so long and I...I mean, I would never..."

Miril got up, turned and headed towards the door.

"Wait!" Lil said, forcing herself to seem calm as a storm whirled inside of her soul.

When Miril turned around, Lil realized she was crying.

Uncertain, she got up and took a few steps towards her. She had no idea what to say or do. Miril froze. She was still crying. She looked as beautiful as ever. Like a goddess.

Lil took another step. Miril seemed to be waiting for her, then she, too, started to move. She daintily held her hand out in front of her and Lil took it in her own.

The two women embraced, holding each other close, their heads resting on each other's shoulders.

"Thanks, Lil. You helped me understand a type of magic that has transformed me, turned me into a different person. Since you've come here, my life has changed."

Lil could sense the years of solitude, the heavy burdens, the strict discipline, and the harsh training that had been Miril's life.

She looked up. The two women's eyes locked. Imperceptibly, Lil's face moved closer to Miril's, who was still crying.

"Miril, you don't need to apologize for how you feel about me."

The priestess looked at her, confused: "Apologize?"

"I..." Lil continued, embarrassed. "I mean, I thought that a priestess couldn't..."

Miril smiled. "Oh, sure. Priests can't have relations with people from the outside, to avoid disrupting their levels of vital energies. But, among each other, I mean...there's no problem."

Lil's jaw dropped. She never would have imagined that such a rule would have been invented. "So, you and the priest...?" she asked tentatively.

The priestess's face lit up with a lively expression: "Oh no! Just because we *can* doesn't mean we *have to*."

"Sure, right, right," Lil hurried to say, feeling that she shouldn't have asked such bold questions.

"And then," Miril added, looking away. "I never had to force myself to repress my emotions towards men. When it came to women, however..." she looked down.

Lil felt her face flush. It must be very difficult for the priestess to be so open with her. She brought her face closer to Miril's and brushed her lips against the woman's mouth. Miril looked up. Her eyes burned, her hands pressed against Lil's back. Something very deep moved in the young woman's soul, something that no man had ever made her feel before.

"Miril, if you want, you can. It would make me happy."

136

"Are you sure, Lil?"

The young woman nodded.

Miril's lips sweetly pressed against Lil's, resting there for a little while. They broke away for a moment, then reunited.

"Oh, Lil…"

Lil abandoned herself to her friend's sweet passion, wondering if it was Miril's first kiss. She wanted to taste the flavor of her mouth, but restrained herself.

They stood, holding each other, their lips chasing after the other's mouth.

"Good night," Miril finally said.

Lil didn't want the priestess to stop with that kiss. But she only replied: "Good night, Miril."

Miril lowered her head and brought the back of Lil's hands to her mouth, kissing them. Then she turned and left.

42

The young apprentice Ilis walked through the palace courtyard, lost in his own thoughts. The master was rather satisfied with him, and it seemed like even the king was happy with the progress they had made. Yet he wasn't too thrilled with the role he was playing.

They had already exterminated almost everyone on that island. Why did they have to terrorize the poor survivors? If their magic rites really did keep the barrier intact and isolate their people from the rest of the world, couldn't there be another way to reach the same goal? He wondered if it would be possible to communicate with the survivors in another manner, to persuade them to do what they wanted. After the storm of rock shards his master Aldin had arranged, he didn't think it was possible to establish peaceful relations with the islanders, but their position of extreme weakness could, perhaps, make them a little more willing to negotiate. Really, what future awaited them if they stayed there alone? Wouldn't they perhaps be better off in the company of those with whom they used to share their lands, once upon a time?

He felt sorry for that man on the island, so lost and isolated. He wished he could help him instead of manipulating him into murdering another person.

A pleasant song roused him from his reflections. Through a window in the room underneath a little arcade, he saw a woman's silhouette, bent over her embroidery. She sang a folk song, one of the tunes his nurse used to sing to him when he was still a little boy.

Intrigued, he opened the small wooden door and walked into the room, where he saw Milia, the king's young wife. He had attended their unusual evening ceremony a few weeks earlier. It had been organized hastily, and the absence of the bride's father made it seem all the more strange.

As the apprentice entered, the song stopped.

"Pardon me, I didn't mean to disturb you, my lady," the young man apologized.

Milia's eyes pierced through him. "You didn't disturb me. And just call me Milia. Until a few weeks ago I was a simple servant girl. I'm having a hard time getting used to my new *royal* rank."

Still standing in the doorway, Ilis observed her cautiously: "I imagine it's a position that has its benefits."

Milia replied sadly: "Oh yes, of course. Many benefits, such as having to satisfy the perversions of a furious madman every night."

Ilis' face flushed. He had never heard anyone talk about King Beanor in that way, much less in a room of the palace.

He came forward, scolding her gently: "What do you mean? Being the king's wife is what every young lady in the kingdom dreams of."

Milia stared at him for a few seconds and then began weeping, covering her face with her hands.

"What's wrong?"

"I hate him!" she explained between sobs. "And I hate this position. It's horrendous. Before I had to work, but I had real friends. I had my family. And...him."

"Him? Him who?" Ilis' eyes grew wide.

Milia just cried harder.

"Shhh!" Ilis motioned for her to stop crying. "They might hear us."

"So what?" Milia retorted, her face wet with tears. "Let them hear me! What, I can't even cry around here?" Her accusatory tone almost made Ilis feel as if he were the cause of all her problems.

Embarrassed, the young man came closer to her. He wanted to help her, but she just kept crying. "Come on, now, maybe we can do something to make you feel better," he said, uncertain.

"What? What? The other wives hate me. They act like the king is just a big toy. They all look at me as if I were the millionth whore the king decided to fuck because he liked her ass. What solution is there? I'm alone, completely alone, and I don't have anyone anymore."

Ilis didn't know what to do, so he just watched her cry. People said the king had decided to marry her merely hours after seeing her for the first time. Now Ilis understood why.

"I'm here for you," he reassured her in a burst of courage, not knowing how those words had managed to come out of his own mouth.

Milia looked at him, her eyes swollen and glassy. "You? You want to be my friend?"

"Of course. It would be an honor."

The girl got up, came towards him and threw her arms around his neck.

43

"I can't take it anymore!" Milia howled. "He's nasty, cruel, perverted and sadistic. I don't want to spend another night in his company."

Despite the thick walls surrounding the underground room, Ilis feared that someone would hear them. "Come on now, calm down."

"Calm down? You don't have to spend your nights satisfying that pig! I'm done! I'd rather die than go on in this way."

Ilis felt his blood freeze. "Now Milia, don't go around saying those sorts of things."

She collapsed onto a leather couch and, with a candle, lit the *formir*, a long pipe in which burned the leaves of a very rare tree. Only the most important dignitaries of the court could enjoy the luxury of smoking.

Milia liked meeting with Ilis in this place, not to mention the pleasure of relaxing in a space far from prying eyes.

After a few puffs, the young woman had calmed down. She inhaled again, held the smoke in her lungs and exhaled.

Milia turned towards Ilis: "Want to try?" she asked, giving him a smile.

"Oh no, no thanks, I don't think my master would be very happy with me if I did."

"Your master isn't here now. It's just me and you. Sure you don't want to? You have no idea how nice it is."

Ilis sat down next to her. "Well, Milia, generally apprentices have to abstain from all vices while they're studying magic."

"Says who?" Milia challenged him, mockingly. "I don't see how a moment of pleasure can cause any problems with your magical education."

Milia took a deep inhale and exhaled in Ilis' direction. He smelled the aroma of the scented smoke.

"Come on, just try it. A little puff won't cause any problems," Milia coaxed, giving him a wink.

Ilis was pretty sure that this was forbidden. But, then again, he had never actually been explicitly told not to smoke. Besides, those leaves were nearly impossible to find, so they weren't going to cause him any long-term problems. Furthermore, a wizard was supposed to learn as much as he could about the real world around him.

He bent down towards the mouthpiece, hesitant.

Milia pushed it between his lips. "Good job. Now breathe in. Hold it, hold it...and now let it all out."

He coughed. Tears came to his eyes and his head immediately started spinning, but he felt much lighter. His problems and anxieties disappeared. Milia, sitting with both her legs up on the couch, looked even more enticing to him.

She took a large mouthful for herself, then handed him the mouthpiece. Ilis didn't hesitate this time.

When the embers of the *formir* stopped burning, both of them laid back with their heads resting on the couch pillows. Ilis, feeling more relaxed than he had ever been, watched Milia's chest rise and fall as she breathed.

"This is so nice. Too bad we both have to go back to our bosses soon. I wish we didn't have to live this way."

Ilis watched her lips open and close.

"You're a wizard. You should be able to put an end to all of this."

Ilis was lost in the brilliant blue of those eyes, as wide as the sky.

"Did you hear what I just said?" Milia scolded him, her voice louder.

The apprentice snapped out of it: "What? Who?"

"I said that you should be able to put an end to all of our suffering. Would you do it? For me?"

What wouldn't I do for her! the young man thought, without understanding what Milia was talking about.

"I'll do whatever you want me to do. What do you want, Milia?" Ilis asked, lost in the darkness of her pupils.

"I want you to free us from the king!"

44

Satisfied, Beanor stroked his unkempt beard. "Interesting. So we'll use this Bashinoir to eliminate the priestess who's the only one still keeping the island's protections active," he summarized.

Obolil, sitting on a chair at the foot of the stairs leading up to the throne, responded: "Exactly, your Majesty. Through the astral dimension, we were able to get to the barrier, and from there we projected a shadow all the way to the island. Using the shadow, we've been able to communicate telepathically with this man, who feels very isolated and alone. So -"

"Yes, yes, I understand. Don't waste my time with all these explanations. When will everything be taken care of?"

Ilis, standing next to Obolil, couldn't resist the impulse to look up towards his master, who was clearly irritated by the interruption.

"Your Majesty," the old wizard explained. "This type of manipulation takes time. If we rush things along too quickly-"

"Words, words, words. For as long as I can remember it's been nothing but words! I've been waiting decades for you to resolve this. How much more time can it possibly take to eliminate two or three survivors?"

Tuirl, sitting to Obolil's left, intervened: "Your Majesty, I think the plan developed by our wizards is excellent on all accounts and, from what they've reported, I don't think we'll be waiting much longer."

Beanor threw his advisor a disgusted look. "Do you have any idea how many times you've asked me to wait? Wait, wait, wait. If you had it your way, I'd do nothing but wait! Your advice has led us nowhere, all we do is waste our lives on this frozen and inhospitable land, just like our ancestors before us. At least Aldin managed to get something done."

Hearing those words, Obolil flushed with humiliation. A loud coughing fit rattled through his battered body.

"Your Majesty," Ilis interjected, unable to restrain himself. The eyes of the king and the advisor stared at him, menacing. It was the first time the young apprentice had ever dared to speak. "It really won't take very long. Communicating with Bashinoir, I can feel the emotions of a man destroyed by guilt, by isolation, and by the thirst for revenge. His ex-wife is now a novice, serving the priestess. He feels alone. I managed to make him believe that what happened was all the priestess's fault and - "

"Did you say that you *communicated* with this Bashinoir?" Beanor asked warily.

"Your Majesty," Obolil interrupted, his voice cracking.

"I wasn't talking to you! Answer me, boy!"

Tuirl saw Obolil grit his teeth.

"Y-yes," Ilis replied. "I followed the master's instructions."

"Ah, very well! So the master considers it unworthy of his time to accompany you on these little trips?"

Ilis placed his hand on the back of the chair. It no longer seemed as if his legs were going to support him. Obolil tried to move his neck back to look at him yet failed, due to a lack of flexibility.

"I work together with the master. He tells me what to do and I do it."

"And how come the wizard Obolil entrusted such a delicate task to a lowly apprentice?"

Ilis lowered his eyes to the ground, embarrassed. His intervention to defend his master had instead backfired, leading to yet another humiliation for Obolil.

The wizard's face was beet red.

Tuirl tried to salvage the situation: "Your Majesty, these complex magical operations require a harmonious team, that only -"

"Yes, yes, I understand. Obolil, Tuirl, if all you intend to do here is talk, you can leave now."

Obolil stood up, trembling and infuriated. Instead of bowing, he merely nodded at the king, then left the room, followed by Tuirl, who walked with his usual composure.

"From now on, you report your progress personally, to me, every day. Do you understand, boy?" the king ordered.

The apprentice, incredibly embarrassed, had no idea how to act. This was his first time ever alone with the king and, even worse, he knew that he had angered his master. "As you wish, your Majesty."

"Listen to me good. Old Obolil never succeeded in getting any kind of results for years. He's so worthless he deserves nothing more than to be tortured in prison. I expect more from you. Only one bastard, the girl he was fucking and a batty virgin live on that island. You need to get rid of them all as soon as possible! Got it? I won't

144

tolerate any more delays. Otherwise, that useless old fart will be the first to pay for it. And I think you can imagine who the second person to suffer will be."

Ilis was petrified. He wanted to tell the king that he and his master worked in symbiosis, that neither of the two would be able to continue on alone.

Beanor, looking at those earnest eyes yearning to express the thoughts behind them, burst out laughing: "Get out of here! But come back tomorrow with your report. If you can take down that cursed barrier, you have the king's word that you can take your pick of the prettiest whores in the southern lands we'll conquer."

Ilis bowed politely and respectfully left the throne room.

He thought about Milia's murderous desires yet again, wondering how badly she wanted the king to die. Absorbed in his own doubts, the apprentice Ilis didn't notice the shadow following him.

45

Bashinoir heard the women laughing in the kitchen. He slowed down, uncertain whether to enter or to stop and eavesdrop. He sensed a strange change in their mood: the two should have been acting more anxious, but instead, they chatted cheerfully.

Outside of the kitchen, he tried to make out what they were talking about. He feared the closeness and intimacy of their relationship. It hurt him to feel so excluded. *Patience. Something's got to give. Soon enough my wife will be all mine again, as she used to be.*

Letting out a sigh, he walked into the kitchen. Miril and Lil stifled their laughter, trying to compose themselves as they greeted him politely. Bashinoir responded coldly. Lil immediately knew something was wrong.

After eating, Miril explained – for the hundredth time – how the rite would be performed.

She sounds like such a prissy little schoolteacher, he thought, disgusted, as he listened to her.

Once she had finished explaining, they headed towards the large room in the Temple, where the women had drawn a wide spiral on the marble floor leading to the sacred fire, which burned in the center. The light of the flames reflected off the mirrors and illuminated the high stretch of columns and frescoes that narrated the history of their people. The pleasant scent of incense hung in the air.

Miril walked along the spiral, singing the words of an ancient mantra of their people. A breeze started to blow through the folds of her green ritual dress. The air became thicker, hard to breath. Out of nowhere, rays of light started to illuminate the room.

Once she reached the fire, she drew the sacred signs, moving her fingers through the air, offering a few ritual elements to the flames, then closed her eyes and waited. The color of the flames changed to a violet hue. She opened her eyes and nodded towards Lil, who began to slowly walk along the spiral. Her hair and dress seemed to be blown by the same wind, which now grew stronger. Lil joined in song with Miril. The intensity of the light inside of the room grew.

Bashinoir held his breath, fascinated by what he saw in front of him, and was tempted to look for a column behind which he could dump the weapon he had hidden in his pants. Maybe he should just forget about the past and let the magic of what was happening around him carry him away.

Lil reached the center of the spiral. She drew other magic signs and offered more elements to the fire.

Miril closed her eyes. Her body became so light she appeared to be floating in the air.

Lil was now in charge of the ritual as the priestess's vital frequencies created a bridge between the past and the present.

Lil looked at Bashinoir and made a sign. He began walking along the spiral. He felt lighter with every step. Fears, anxieties, tensions, and resentment gradually disappeared. His limbs felt less heavy as his flesh, blood and bone seemed to give way to a light blue vapor.

When he reached the spot where the two women stood, the walls of the room began to turn transparent. The priestess's body lost its consistency and solidity.

Bashinoir looked around, mesmerized. For a second, he thought he could see the sea. It was as if he were on top of a hill that gently sloped towards the water.

The cold blade in his pocket, however, felt even heavier. He wanted to get rid of it, but now it was too late. Where could he throw it without being seen?

The priestess's body rose a few inches from the ground. Her face, turned upwards, was illuminated by a ray of sunlight coming from the ceiling. Bashinoir admired her, thunderstruck. He wanted to entrust his spirit to her, as he used to.

He saw Lil's face out of the corner of his eye. She was looking at Miril with a gaze full of awe, devotion, surprise, and something else he didn't want to admit he saw.

Love! She's in love with the priestess! She loves her, she wants to stay with her. The thought pierced through his heart. *And now I'll lose her forever!*

He thought about how the two exchanged smiles, how they chattered on in low voices, how they traded intense gazes. *How did I not see this before?*

He couldn't accept it. *No, it can't be true! If it were just us two on this island, we could leave this cursed Temple forever. I'd finish building our house. We'd have children. She'd be happy with me!*

147

He sighed. *I have to do it!* He took out the weapon. When they had gone over the details of the ritual beforehand, he had guessed that Miril wouldn't be able to defend herself. He leapt towards her. She didn't withdraw an inch. He lifted the knife to her chest, then hesitated. Suspended in the air, illuminated by the sunlight, she was so beautiful, luminous, *divine.*

"Bashinoir!" Lil's terrified scream echoed through the air. "Please, don't do it. Please, I'm begging you!" she pleaded, coming towards him slowly.

"Lil, you don't understand. She's the reason why. It's her fault they all died. She didn't protect us. She's selfish. And she stole you away from me."

"No, that's not true, and you know that. She has always done everything she could to protect us. *You're* the one who's grown distant from me over these past months. We could have grown closer together to one another, been friends, we could have helped each other through our everyday burdens, but you were too proud to accept the path I had to take. But now...now we can learn from our mistakes. Please, Bashinoir, put down that knife."

The ritual song intoned by Miril, suspended in the air, grew in intensity. Sunlight now flooded the entire room. He could smell the sea and hear the sound of the waves.

Bashinoir had tears in his eyes. "I'm sorry, Lil, but we need to go home. We can have beautiful children, live a beautiful life." He lifted his hand in the air, ready to deal the fatal blow, and brought it down violently. Lil jumped in front of the woman's body, shielding it. Bashinoir saw the knife plunge into the flesh above his wife's breast. Horrified, he pulled out the bloody blade. "Lil!" he screamed. "I didn't-" but an arrow pierced through his heart and his body disappeared.

The two women fell on the wet grass of a meadow. Miril, noticing Lil's wound, immediately came to her aid. Watching the red lake devour the young woman's snow white dress, she couldn't hold back her tears, which mixed with the blood as they fell. She pulled the dress away to get a better look at the wound. When she lifted her head to scream, she saw four archers who, their bows tense, had surrounded them.

148

46

Beanor thrusted savagely.

"Oh yes, your Majesty. Nobody makes me feel as good as you do."

Satisfied, Beanor groaned, continuing to push wildly, his face a mask of sweat. He pounced upon the girl's neck, biting her in a rage.

"Oh, your Majesty, you drive me crazy! Oh, oh, I can't hold it back anymore. AAAAAH!"

Milia lifted her feet above the king's waist, squeezing him in between her thighs as her body shivered wildly.

"Ah, your Majesty! Bite me again! You know how much I love it when you hurt me!"

Beanor sought her neck again. Simply touching it with his lips made Milia scream with pleasure. Beanor, unable to resist, came inside of her. His orgasm was accompanied by gasps, grunts, and bellows.

"Your Majesty! How did you become such a passionate lover?" Milia congratulated him.

He rolled over next to her. She came closer, caressing his chest. The king turned to the other side, closing his eyes. A few moments later, he fell into a deep sleep.

Milia poured out some of the water from the glass placed on her bedside table. She took out a slender purple ampoule and emptied the contents into the glass. Then she grabbed an elegantly decorated box and turned towards Beanor, opening it underneath his nostrils. She waited a few seconds, then hid it under her table. She rested her head against the pillow and closed her eyes.

Beanor thrashed in his sleep. He turned to his right side, but a coughing fit suddenly tormented him. He woke up and tried to lift his head from the pillow, succeeding only on the second attempt.

"El-Milia...I don't feel well."

Milia pretended to wake up all of a sudden.

"Oh, your Majesty! What's wrong? Your face is covered in sweat!"

"Water. Give me some water, now. I'm dying of thirst!"

"But of course. Here you are," she responded, handing him the glass.

He lifted his head to drink. Beanor downed it all in one gulp, immediately feeling better. He sat up. Milia caressed his face as Beanor stared at her breasts.

He wanted to lift his hand and touch them, but once again he was consumed in a sudden coughing fit. He started to spit blood out onto the sheets. Horrified, he looked in front of him, then turned towards Milia. Suspicious and confused, his eyes flitted between the young woman's face to the glass of water.

He coughed again, hurling the blood towards Milia's face, who screamed in horror. He brought his hand to her neck, trying to choke her, and she screamed more from fear than the weak pressure.

The men guarding the king's bedroom, who had been sleeping up until that moment, stirred as soon as the girl started screaming. One sat up and smiled, envying the king's good fortune. He imagined what it would be like to rape one of those splendid wives, and the sweet fantasy lulled him back to sleep.

The apprentice Ilis slipped right by him and, walking swiftly and silently, reached the royal bedroom, closing the door behind him. He helped the girl who, trembling and covered in blood, had managed to wriggle free. They watched the king squirm and gasp on the bed.

"Try to calm down, now. We're leaving," he told her, caressing her.

Beanor brought his hands to his throat, twisting and turning, until falling at the feet of the two who were on their way out. The door opened and the wizard Obolil appeared in the entrance.

"Ainta sume ardà mal..." Ilis started to pronounce.

But the wizard was quicker: "Zapat!" he yelled, accompanying the spell with a sweeping gesture of his hand.

Ilis and Milia were thrown against the wall. Milia hit it so hard she lost consciousness. Ilis got tangled up with a candelabra and fell to the ground, dazed.

The king started gurgling. A yellow foam spilled from his mouth.

Obolil looked around him and saw the glass on the bedside table. He hastened towards the bed, stepping over the king, and took the glass in his hand, balancing against the bed so he wouldn't lose his footing. Then he turned towards Ilis, furious. "Zermis ibà coras mitas ornì del!"

King Beanor stopped gurgling: the air once again began flowing through his lungs.

Ilis got up and ran towards Milia to see if she was still alive. Holding the girl in his arms, he pronounced a powerful spell right as the wizard tried to attack him. Falling to the ground, Obolil yelled: "Guards!"

The two men outside of the door finally understood their presence was necessary. They ran into the room, where they saw, terrified, the king and the wizard on the ground as the apprentice, holding the young wife in his arms, looked at them with a menacing gaze. The eldest guard ordered the other: "Run for help." The other guard flew out of the room before Ilis could convince him otherwise.

Tuirl was woken by the guard running through the corridors, asking for help to save the king's life. He came out of his room and headed towards the royal apartments. When he entered, he saw Obolil near the entrance, looking at him with glassy eyes, unable to move. Beanor, covered in blood and writhing with seizures, managed to beg: "Help me." In the back of the room, the apprentice Ilis was bent over the king's beautiful wife. It looked like he was trying to resuscitate her.

Tuirl ran and knelt down next to the king. Staring him in the eye, he took a dagger from his pocket, raised it in the air and lowered it violently towards his heart, right as another person walked into the room.

"Kill him," Aleia ordered the archer standing next to her. The soldiers standing behind them held their breath. The arrow pierced the advisor's heart, who froze for a second with the dagger in mid-air. Then his hand, still gripping the weapon, fell over the king's body, piercing his chest. Surrendering, Tuirl fell over his own arm, pushing the blade downwards. Beanor let out his last breath.

Ilis got up: "Arbiah mazrel tofà..."

The queen pointed at Milia: "Stop, apprentice. Or she dies."

There are too many of them, the young man thought, looking at the archers standing with their bows drawn.

"The king is dead. Long live the queen," the wizard Obolil croaked from the ground. The guards knelt in front of Aleia.

"Tie them up," she ordered. "And prepare the pyre for the execution."

151

Galactic Energies

Discover Galactic Energies on Amazon Kindle

http://www.amazon.com/dp/B00E3VTR1K/

The **artificial intelligences** of DataCom are trying to save the planet... by exterminating the human race.

Aurelia finds her perfect man: a **robot**.

The space explorer Captain Arcot sacrifices his life for an impossible conquest, the heart of Vril the **vampire queen**.

A **shape-shifting mutant** ignites the erotic desires of the galactic police officer who's been tracking her down.

Alessio fights against **corruption** in a universe of his own creation.

An innocent man is forced to submit to the **domination** of a ruthless prison director.

A king who's forgotten his own past wanders through a **magical dimension** where he discovers his own history.

Two souls separated after one abandons the other meet again in **another life**.

In an exciting **virtual reality** game, the hunter of the fearsome black widow becomes her prey.

Ranked #1 in WIRED's Self Published Books

A Highly Rated Read Voted To The Following Positions on Goodreads:
#1 in Great Fun Science Fiction & Fantasy
#1 in Parallel Universes
#1 in Greatest horror/fantasy books ever!
#1 in Favorite Fantasy Books
#1 in Indie Novellas, Novelettes, and Short Stories
#1 in Indie/Self-Published Books
#1 in Anthologies you just HAVE TO READ
#1 in Best Genuinely Unusual Fiction
#2 in Books that most influenced you
#3 in Amazing Paranormal Books
#7 in Best Indie Fantasy Books
#7 in Awsome Action
#7 in Best Anthologies

Discover Galactic Energies on Amazon Kindle

http://www.amazon.com/dp/B00E3VTR1K/

The Branches of Time – Volume II

Don't miss the second volume of The Branches of Time
Subscribe to Luca Rossi's mailing list
http://www.lucarossi369.com/2014/04/mailing-list.html

The Author

Research, science, science fiction and high technology: this is the world of Luca Rossi, and the main themes that run through his literary work.

He believes the internet provides a tool to bring people together and make the world a more open, fair and democratic place.

In 2013 he published *Galactic Energies,* a collection of short stories set in a universe where not just the laws of physics, but also the laws of eros, passion, desire and the spirit are a little different than our own.

He was born in Turin on April 15th, 1977. He likes to ride his bike, take walks through nature and spend most of his free time with his family.

Visit the website: www.lucarossi369.com/search/label/EN
sign up on the mailing list
  www.lucarossi369.com/2014/04/mailing-list.html
contact him by email: luca@lucarossi369.com
or follow him on Facebook
  www.facebook.com/LucaRossiAuthor
Twitter
  twitter.com/AuthorLRossi
 Google+
  plus.google.com/+LucaRossiAuthor/
Pinterest
  pinterest.com/lucarossi369/
Linkedin
  www.linkedin.com/in/lucarossiauthor
 Goodreads:
  www.goodreads.com/author/show/6863455.Luca_Rossi
Instagram
  instagram.com/lucarossi369
Amazon
  amazon.com/author/lucarossi

Printed in Great Britain
by Amazon.co.uk, Ltd.,
Marston Gate.